GRANITE GORGE

A Dan Courtwright Mystery

Other Books by Paul Wagner :

Dan Courtwright Mysteries
Danger: Falling Rocks
Bones of the Earth
Holes in the Ground

Artisan Public Relations
Wine Sales and Distribution
Wine Marketing and Sales

Lecture Series:
The Instant Sommelier (Great Courses)
A History of Wine in 10 Glasses (Audible)

GRANITE GORGE

PAUL WAGNER

A Dan Courtwright Mystery

Published by Albicaulis Books

*To Chip and Bill, and all the other people
who put in days and weeks and months
over the years in the mountains on trail crews,
paid or unpaid—with your chain saws, bucksaws,
rock bars, McLeods, picks, shovels, rakes, loppers
and extractigators, this one is for you*

It had been five long and hot hours of bushwhacking to get from last night's campsite to this point—pushing through dense thickets of huckleberry oak and white thorn, wandering back and forth through granite mazes and up and down a few class III scrambles. Ranger Dan Courtwright had climbed through and over too many downed trees to count. He now stopped to catch his breath and let his body recover, at least for a moment.

It was hot. The kind of hot and dry you only get at the lower elevations of the Sierra, where the sun radiates off the rock surfaces to cook you even in the shade. Sweat was dripping down his face, the combination of salt and sunscreen burning his eyes, splashing down on his sunglasses, and his shirt was soaked enough to make it hard to wipe them off. The only saving grace was that he was still above the 5,000-foot elevation level and didn't need to worry about poison oak. That, and he'd only seen two rattlesnakes all day.

But now things opened up in front him. Once he had solved the riddle of how to clamber up onto the massive granite bench on the right-hand side of the canyon, it looked like he could hike it for at least half a mile downstream. It was the only path forward, but it looked good—a wide natural stone sidewalk sloping exactly where he wanted to go: down the canyon. It certainly came as a relief. And that might even be a slight breath of a breeze that he was feeling.

To his right the dark gray mounding sheets of rock sloped up steeply into towering cliffs a thousand feet high, covered with brush and trees that jutted out into the sky, clinging to life on the bare stone. He craned his neck to gaze up at them and wonder how those trees ever got enough nutrients to live up there.

To the left the charcoal granite dropped precipitously more than a hundred feet down into a dark, narrow channel that had room for the river, and not much else. There were deep pools, and massive piles of boulders that the river sometimes went over, sometimes under. It was a single slot eroded along a fracture in the bedrock of the canyon. There was no room on either side for a man to walk—only cliffs, deep blue-green pools, an occasional flash of white water, and massive boulders. He could hear the river down there, grumbling away as it worked its way down the gorge, echoing in the granite walls.

Looking down the canyon, Dan could see that the end of the bench gradually dropped away out of sight. According to the topo map, that would leave him back near the level of the river where it came out of the narrow channel. He was hopeful that the terrain there would be easier to hike. And maybe a flat place to camp that night. That was important because by then he was going to be ready to stop.

He was alone. Few people ever ventured down into this remote canyon, and those who did usually emerged covered with bruises, scratches and scrapes. He had a few of those already, including a nasty gash on his leg from the stub of a broken limb on a tree he had to climb over. When it was time to stop, that one would require some attention. Right now it just added a splash of red color to his dusty brown right shin and a small stain on the sock below.

He finished off the last of his water, adjusted his hat on his head, gave his shoulders a shrug to settle his pack, and started hiking down the granite bench, deeper into the canyon, down into the granite gorge.

chapter 1

It was a phone call from a fisherman that started Ranger Dan Courtwright on the trail. While working phone duty in the Summit ranger station one day, Dan had taken the call that piqued his curiosity. The guy wanted to know about an old trail that was supposed to run the length of the Mokelumne Canyon. And there was something odd about the way he was asking the questions.

Dan didn't have much information to offer. While he was on the phone, he had looked at the topo map, and seen that the river tracked through twenty or thirty miles of wilderness. There were at least five trails leading down into that canyon, but none of them seemed to connect with any of the others. And even though Dan had worked in the Stanislaus National Forest for the past four years, he had never even been on the other side of Highway 4. Not his department, as his boss liked to say.

As he talked with the guy on the phone, Dan made eye contact with his assistant, Doris. Approaching retirement age, Doris had a vast amount of local knowledge that often surprised Dan with its quantity and its seemingly random collection of data, both accurate and inaccurate.

As the tall ranger towered over her, Doris followed Dan's finger to where it was pointing on the map that lay out on the counter. She leaned her head in close to the map, where her thick wire-rimmed glasses could make out the details if she squinted. Then she straightened back up again and met Dan's gaze.

She rolled her eyes, made a grimace with her mouth, and shook her head slowly back and forth.

Dan shot her a questioning look, and Doris responded with another slow shake of her head, her lips pressed tightly together.

The man on the phone persisted with a few more questions to Dan, and Dan had to apologize. "I'm sorry, but I just don't know very much about that area," he said. "It's right on the edge of our jurisdiction…"

The guy on the phone interrupted him. "That's the same answer I got from El Dorado," he said with a note of annoyance. "It's right between the two of you, and nobody knows much about it."

Dan explained that the two trails that entered the canyon from his side were both quite primitive and hadn't been maintained in years. "It would be a real adventure to hike down there," he said. "But I would not suggest that unless you are really experienced. And careful."

"Yeah," the man responded. "That's what El Dorado said, too."

Dan took down the man's name and number and promised him to do a little research on the area and call him back.

"El Dorado said that, too," the man replied. "That was about a week ago…"

Dan smiled to himself. He would make a point of doing better than that.

Once he got off the phone, Dan turned to Doris.

Doris shook her head again. "That is the back of beyond," she said grimly. "You could go down there and disappear, and nobody would even know where to look for you. It's happened."

Dan asked if she knew anyone who had hiked into the canyon.

Doris waved at him dismissively. "The last time I heard about anyone down there they came out looking like the dog's breakfast," she said. "We try to discourage that kind of thing. The SAR teams have enough to do these days without looking for people who wander down there. And not finding them."

Dan smiled. "So when was this?"

"Well, the group was years ago," Doris said. "They were going to find the old cabin somehow… Monty Wolfe's. But they never made it. That's really rugged country. Somebody broke a leg or something and we had to send in a helicopter to get them out of there."

"Wow." Dan was impressed. "I'll have to check it out. That's the kind of place I like."

Doris fixed him with a stare, her short gray curls framing her face like a tight cloud. "Maybe. I'm not sure anybody likes it. Besides, you might want to check with Steve Matson about that," she said. "It's not exactly on his priority list."

Steve was their boss, and Dan knew from experience that Doris knew more than she was telling him. He also knew that if he kept quiet, she would probably keep talking.

It didn't take long. Doris began to straighten the maps behind her in the racks. Then she turned to Dan again.

"That whole thing with the cabin is a mess," she said. "And I think that Steve wishes it would all just evaporate…"

Dan waited a bit longer. The rest would come.

"But those preservation people think it's the cat's meow," she continued, changing her tone to mimic a kind of grand oratory: "It is an essential part of our region's history, and must be preserved at all costs!" She blew out her cheeks, which was about as close to Doris ever came to swearing.

Doris glanced at the clock and then turned away from him. "Time to get some work done around here," she said over her shoulder. "You can read all about it online…there are lots of stories in the local papers."

Dan decided he would do just that.

chapter 2

That evening at home, Dan turned on his computer to check his email, and found a note from Doris. "Thought you might want to read up about this, so here are a few links…"

Dan grinned. Doris just couldn't help herself helping others, especially him.

He clicked on the first link and found a news story about a lingering controversy between the Forest Service and a group of preservationists. On one side, the Forest Service was concerned that Monty Wolfe's cabin was becoming a destination and a campsite—an attractive nuisance in a very isolated part of the wilderness, and something that was an illegal use in that wilderness. On a trip down there a few years ago, they had found food stored in the cabin, and a lock that they couldn't open on the door.

On the other side, the preservationists were furious that the Forest Service had removed some parts of the cabin, which is a historic structure and must be preserved, and put their own lock on the door to prevent access. They claimed the Forest Service had damaged a building of historic interest and value.

Both sides were quoted extensively, and while the story was from quite a few years ago, Dan could still identify the official Forest Service language as coming straight out of the policy manual. And both sides sounded annoyed with the other. The whole thing shined a light on that odd concept of "arrested decay" that the Forest Service uses to manage places like this. It's not an easy concept to explain, Dan thought. You let things decay, but you protect them while they decay…

But the link didn't include any photos, or indication of where the cabin might be, other than down in the canyon. It did, however, include a note as a follow-up to the story. In this case, the Forest Service explained that they had sealed the door and chimney to prevent animals from entering the cabin, and to make it more secure.

The Monty Wolfe Society had complained to friends in higher places than the Amador Ranger Station, and now there were plans to restore the damaged portions of the cabin to historic accuracy, thanks to a couple of letters from the local congressman to the head of the USFS.

Dan smiled. He knew how much this would have pained the Forest Service… and he decided that he was going to have to learn more about this cabin. Maybe the next link would have more.

A group calling itself the Monty Wolfe Society had pitched a few stories to local papers, and these included a few photos of a rustic cabin, apparently built in the 1920s. From these articles, Dan pulled out more information, piece by piece. As he read more, he found a note in one of the stories that the USGS no longer includes the cabin on their topo maps.

That made him curious. And that led him to another search, and after quite a few minutes, led him to a set of GPS coordinates for Monty Wolfe's Cabin in another one of the links Doris had sent him.

Dan plotted them on a map and realized that they couldn't be accurate. They were high on a ridge and far from the river, nowhere near where the cabin was supposed to be.

Then he found a mention of a second cabin, with GPS

coordinates for that one. But that one was described as no longer in existence. It had burned down decades ago, and besides, it wasn't the real cabin. Dan marked it down on his map and kept searching.

He found a fragment of an old Sierra Club map that identified the location of the cabin, but it was just a small section of a topo map, without any context or coordinates. There was no way to tell where it was. Dan consequently spent twenty minutes comparing contour lines, curves in the river, elevations, and a number of other clues between the Sierra Club scrap and his own topo maps before he finally decided that he knew where the cabin was. Or at least, where it might be.

Which was the middle of nowhere. Deep down in the Mokelumne Canyon, at least a thousand feet below any of the trailheads, and with no trails that came closer than a couple of miles to the location. In the summer, it would be a hot and brutal bushwhack. And in winter, with the massive snowfall, it would have taken days and days to get anywhere at all.

Whoever build that cabin wanted solitude, Dan thought.

Which led him to read the story of Monty Wolfe, the man who built the cabin.

From what Dan read online, Monty was quite a character. This led to more searches online, and more conflicting information. The details of his early life were a bit cloudy, especially because Monty liked to tell stories. He claimed to have come West on one of the last wagon trains on the Oregon Trail, and served as a scout for the US Army fighting Pancho Villa in Mexico. He spent time in jail for theft and managed to get exonerated for a couple of other offenses that were something between serious felonies and practical jokes. He went by at least two different names, and while he had described himself as a committed loner, he had a wife and children who not only survived him, but whose descendants were still alive today.

But Monty's family didn't live with him in that cabin. They lived in Stockton, and never visited Monty. And he didn't visit them much, as far as Dan could tell.

At the same time, there was no doubt that Monty Wolfe was a force of nature. Visitors to the cabin found an amazing amount of heavy log construction work as well as heavy equipment, all carried there by Monty himself, including a cast iron stove. Dan shuddered to think of the effort it must have taken to carry that chunk of iron into the canyon.

Monty Wolfe trapped animals, chopped firewood, and lived on the land for many years. And then one spring, in 1940, Monty just plain disappeared. The cabin was empty, and it simply looked as if Monty had gone for a walk. There was food on the table, his fishing rod was missing, and he had never returned. In the intervening eighty years, nobody had ever found hide nor hair of Monty Wolfe.

Dan had to admit it. He was hooked. And that was before he clicked on the last link—a news story about a woman who had disappeared without a trace, and whose car had been found, with all her valuables inside, at the trailhead that would lead down towards Monty Wolfe's cabin.

That woman was from Columbia, just down the hill from the ranger station.

chapter 3

The next morning Dan was on the phone to Steve Matson to follow up on a couple of reports that Matson had wanted him to write. Dan was careful to point out how much progress he was making, and to assure Steve that he would have the reports on his desk by the day after tomorrow—two days early.

At the end of the conversation, right when Dan felt he had Matson as close to happy as it was possible to get him, Dan mentioned the phone call about a cabin down in the Mokelumne Canyon.

Matson replied with eloquent silence. No comments or questions, just silence, as if the phone had gone dead.

Dan knew that with his boss this wasn't a good sign, but he plunged on ahead, hoping to break through Matson's obvious resistance.

"I've always been interested in the early pioneers here," Dan said. "When was the last time anyone went down there? Seems like that cabin would be worth a visit…" his voice trailed off.

At the other end of the phone, Matson waited for a while, and then finally spoke. "Not on company time," he said firmly.

"I know we've got some trail crews coming in, and I was thinking…" Dan continued.

"Not as part of any project moving forward," Matson

interrupted. "And just so you know, Monty Wolfe wasn't anything close to a pioneer. The guy lived down there in the 1920s and 30s. Not exactly the Gold Rush. Ten years later and he could have been a '49er—a 'nineteen' '49er."

"Still," Dan insisted. "I know that whole canyon is wilderness now. But where does it fit in to our management plan? I mean, we do have some trails down there…"

"Class one," Matson replied. "Minimally developed. And that's how they will stay."

"Okay. Got it," Dan agreed, trying to sound as cooperative as possible. "Any idea when we did any maintenance down there?"

"Not since I've been here," Matson assured him. "And I don't see any reason to do any now, either. That whole area is as primitive as it can be, and it's going to stay that way—both because we want it to stay that way, and because with the kind of funding we have, that whole damn canyon is the last place we would ever spend any time, effort or money."

"Got it," Dan said. He thought this over.

"Anything else?" Matson asked, although his tone of voice indicated that he really hoped Dan didn't have anything else.

But since Dan was already this far along, he pressed to the end.

"I was just reading about that cabin," he said. "I might try to hike down there sometime…"

"Other side of the river," Matson said. "Not in our forest. It's in El Dorado. If you want to hike there, go ahead. I can't stop you, obviously, but not on company time."

While Dan took this in, Matson continued. "If there's one piece of good news in all of this, it's that the damn cabin is in the El Dorado. So they get to deal with it. And we don't have to deal with it."

"Yeah," Dan agreed. "I mean, we have two trails that go down into that canyon…"

"And those trails do not cross the river," Matson finished Dan's sentence for him. "Those two trails are minimally developed and minimally maintained. And they will stay that way. If you want to maintain some trails, we have plenty in the Emigrant that get tons of use. And we have both budgets and plans to do that. You have the list."

Dan could tell that Steve Matson was getting angry because his sentences were getting longer. He figured it was about time to call a retreat.

"No, I understand," he said. "I was just curious, since we got this phone call about it, and I wanted to get back to the guy with some information."

"He's welcome to take the trails down there, but he should be prepared for…" Here Matson paused to quote the exact Forest Service language… "route finding challenges and obstacles."

Dan gave a slight chuckle. "Okay, that's what I'll tell him. And I will get you those reports…"

"Thank you." Matson's curt tone told Dan all he needed to know about discussing the topic further.

Dan hung up the phone and walked out of his office. Doris was at the counter, and the big topo map was still laid out in front of her. Her eyes followed Dan as he walked over to the map and took a closer look. As he peered at the tightly spaced contour lines on the steep sides of the canyon, Dan could feel Doris' eyes still on him. And maybe a slightly disapproving look on her face.

chapter 4

That afternoon Dan was delighted to see Sheriff Cal Healey's patrol vehicle pull into the parking lot. He and Cal had worked together a number of times, and always enjoyed the partnership—even if some of the work had involved some pretty ugly situations. Cal was the closest thing Dan had to a best friend, and Cal's wife Maggie seemed to consider Dan a lost soul worth saving. Which Dan didn't mind at all, since it got him invited to many delicious dinners at their house.

As Dan finished off another page of data for the report to Steve Matson, he could hear Cal's voice out in the main office, asking if his holiness were receiving visitors today.

Dan chuckled and was already on his way out when Doris stuck her head in.

"You heard?" she asked, with a smile.

Dan nodded and followed her out into the office.

"It's good to see that Tuolumne County Sheriffs don't have anything better to do on a day like today than get in the way of federal employees as we try to get our important work done, serving the public," Dan said.

Cal laughed and shook Dan's hand. "Good to see you, too," he said.

After the required pleasantries, Dan asked Cal why he had

stopped in.

"We've got a report of an abandoned car up by Dodge Ridge. Seems like it's been there for a couple of weeks now." Cal said.

"That sounds important," Dan said sarcastically.

"Being a ranger, you would think that," Cal shot back. "But as a Sheriff, I ran the plates and found out it belongs to someone who has been missing for quite a while. A lot more than two weeks…"

"Okay," Dan surrendered. "You win. It is important. Or at least interesting. What do you need from us?"

"Remember that woman who went missing about a couple of years ago up here?" Cal asked. "Carol Lawlor? She came up here to the lake with a friend, and the friend got a ride back with someone else?"

Dan nodded. "Yep. I read about her last night. Although I wasn't here when it happened—I was working trail crews that summer. They found her car over by Hermit Valley, but no sign of her…"

"Yeah," Cal agreed. "That's right. Her purse, her keys… everything was still in the car. Like she just fell off the face of the earth. And no sign or word of her ever since. Only now it turns out that the abandoned car up here belongs to her… and nobody seems to know how it got here."

Dan and Doris looked at each other.

"Well, I don't think she had a family. Who inherited her things?" Doris asked.

Cal shook his head. "Nope. Ran a bookstore down in Columbia. No kids. No next of kin. Left all of her stuff to the Yosemite Conservancy…"

Dan shrugged. "They would have just sold everything off…."

"Not yet," Cal corrected him. "They haven't done anything. The store is still there, still closed. And her house is still there. Until she is officially declared deceased, nobody can do anything…"

"So, meanwhile, somebody stole the car," Dan said.

"That's what I am trying to figure out," Cal said. "Because when she disappeared, we put it in storage at the tow yard, running up a bill for a few weeks. Then somebody suggested that we just take it over to her house… since she wasn't going to pay the bill."

"That sounds way too reasonable," Dan said. "Which one of you guys came up with that one? Taking money out of your own pocket? Hard to believe."

Cal shot him a look. "The lawyer for the Yosemite Conservancy suggested it, if you want to know the truth," he said.

Dan laughed. "I figured it wasn't you guys. And then somebody stole it from the house? Or did someone from the Yosemite group borrow it?"

"Well, that's the odd part," Cal said. "The lawyer tells me he's got all the keys, and no nobody has driven it. It's not insured… you know how lawyers are about that stuff. But it doesn't really matter, because they took the battery out of the car when they took it over to her house… just in case."

Dan burst out laughing. "Somebody stole the car and drove it away with a dead battery?"

Cal smiled. "See? I knew you would want to know about this … and no, not a dead battery. A non-existent battery. There's a difference."

"Oh yeah," Dan agreed. Now he was curious. "Hey, do you want me to go up there with you?"

Cal shook his head. "No need, even though your expertise in Grand Theft Auto might be helpful. I'll go up there and check it out. Make sure the battery really is gone."

Doris slowly shook her head back and forth. "That is really

crazy…"

"Let us know what you find out," Dan said.

Cal looked out the window. "Nice day for a drive up here—battery or not."

Dan gave a quick glance over to Doris, and then asked Cal "Do you have a minute?"

Cal nodded.

Dan opened the door and walked Cal out to his car. "Do you know anything about the trails down into the Mokelumne Canyon?" he asked Cal.

Cal squinted into the sun as he looked up at Dan. "Are you looking for some exercise?" he asked.

"Maybe," Dan answered. "I'm just curious."

"Jesus," Cal said. "I haven't been down there in a long time…"

Dan watched his friend pause briefly as he searched his memory.

"I bet the last time I was down there was back in high school," Cal said. "A friend and I hiked up over the ridge behind Mt. Reba and hiked way the hell down into that canyon to go fishing." His eyes drifted off to follow a car pulling a camping trailer down the highway. "We figured it was so isolated that the fishing would be great."

"How was it?" Dan asked.

"Good, but not great," Cal admitted. "But I remember the hike down. We must have been carrying forty- or fifty-pound packs, and when we sat down at the bottom our legs were vibrating like sewing machines…" He made a vibrating motion with his hands.

Dan laughed. "Been there," he said.

"And then the second day, this guy just takes off downriver to go fishing, and I never saw him again," Cal said.

"What?" Dan's face contorted in surprise.

"Said he was coming back for lunch," Cal said. "Never showed. By about four or five o'clock, I figured I'd better go get help, so I hoofed it on up out of there. Waved down a passing car that just happened to be driven by the wife of one of the Sheriff Deputies back then. They put me up in a hotel for night, and we all rode back down there on horses the next day…"

He left the story there.

Dan smiled. "And?"

"Oh, the guy was right there in camp. He'd just been fishing all day and forgot what time it was. He was pissed at me for panicking, and I was pissed at him for not showing up on time. And the deputy was probably pissed at both of us…"

"Sounds like a great trip," Dan said dryly.

Cal opened the door to his car and got in. "We didn't talk a lot on the hike back out," he admitted. "But that is some wild country down there. If you ever wanted to disappear, that would be a good place to do it. "

"Yeah," Dan agreed. "I've heard that. Of course, things might have changed since then. What was that, fifty years ago?"

Cal laughed. "Almost. Back when you were in diapers," he said, and drove off.

chapter 5

When Dan went back into the ranger station, Doris was waiting for him.

"You know, Dan, if you really want to know more about that canyon, there is a woman who writes for the local paper who might know more," she said. "I seem to remember her writing a few things about Monty Wolfe, years ago."

Dan asked for the woman's name, and Doris gave it to him. But then she showed Dan her computer monitor. "She still writes things from time to time," Doris said, pointing to the screen. "I bet you could just write her and ask her."

Dan leaned in over Doris' shoulder and copied down the email address at the bottom of the article. That would give him something to do this evening.

"And there's that guy up in Tahoe who is trying to revive the old Tahoe to Yosemite Trail," she continued. "I think he has hiked most of that trail, and he even posts videos of some of the sections."

Again, Dan leaned in while Doris did some quick navigation on the internet. Within a few minutes she had a new site up on the screen, and Dan wrote down the details. The site seemed to have massive amounts of information, although maybe not so much on the Mokelumne. In fact, it described the section as the most difficult part of the whole Tahoe to Yosemite Trail.

"And there is a group of 'Friends of the Monty Wolfe Cabin,'" Doris went on. "But I am not quite sure how to get a hold of them."

Dan noticed that Doris was still punching keys on her computer.

"I'll copy all of these websites and email addresses and send them to you," she said to Dan.

"Thanks," Dan said. Then he crumpled up the paper in his hands that had all of his notes on it. "That would make things a lot easier."

"But you know," Doris continued. "I knew Carol Lawlor. She was a lovely person. And I have never felt comfortable driving past that bridge, knowing that her car was found there…"

"How did you know her?" Dan asked.

"Her bookstore was a little island of sanity up here," Doris explained. "A quiet place for thoughtful people. And she was the one who made it that way."

Dan looked at Doris and saw the beginnings of tears in her eyes.

"She deserved something better than to just disappear like that," Doris said quietly. "And she loved that bookstore. She would never have left it like that. Something terrible must have happened to her that she never came back. They never found her…her body."

Dan murmured an agreement, and then left Doris to her memories.

That evening Dan sent out a few emails from the list that Doris had sent him. Two came back as undeliverable email addresses, so he crossed those off his list.

But from one hiker he got a quick response. "There are no trails left down there," the email read. "It sure used to be part of the Tahoe Yosemite Trail, but now it's almost impassable. Nothing to follow. You'd better really know what you're doing if you go down there.

It's a complete bushwhack, and you need real route-finding skills."

Dan wrote a note of thanks, and by the time he had finished, there a was a ping in his inbox.

He was surprised to see an email from the local writer who had written about Monty Wolfe.

"Hi Dan

What I wrote about Monty Wolfe was so long ago, I don't remember what I wrote. He had strong legs, like beer kegs. He liked the ladies and hung out at Tamarack where there was once a bar. Full of stories of derring-do. He had a couple affairs with married women and one husband swore he'd kill him. And a friend of mine once caught him with a woman outside in the open air and discreetly moved away.

People often wondered if his stories were true. He also hung out in Tuolumne County under a different name, but I can no longer remember what it was. I think it was Fred something. He told someone he'd been in "service." He may have been a deserter. Or others speculated he had committed crimes of some sort and arranged his life so as not to be caught.

He wandered at some point into Amador County. But for most of his time, he stayed in Calaveras County. He could hike the steep canyons and snowshoe through heavy drifts of snow and never seemed daunted by the cold or inclement weather. He had two cabins. One in the woods and one on the river where he regularly fished. He also had pet cats who starved to death when he disappeared.

No one ever found his body. A guy by the name of O'Henry also worked the Enterprise. He came behind me and dug up more information than I had. You might check that out. I don't know where you'd find his article, however. He had to have surgery once and a couple who befriended him, I forgot their name, of course, took him to a hospital and took care of him while he recuperated.

About his disappearance, speculation has it that an avalanche of snow toppled him down a steep bank and covered him up. Maybe during a thaw his body washed down the river.

Monty actually carried a heavy cookstove for miles by foot up to his main cabin. He often took what he wanted, or "borrowed" from locals, as he considered it. The cabin he built was made from heavy logs if I remember correctly. Since I can no longer remember stuff, you can have fun with this information… and if you wish to call me, my number is 209 XXX XXXX. Land line. But I doubt I could add anything."

Dan smiled. He would have to give Mary a call. Tomorrow. After he finished those reports for Matson. And called that guy back, the one who started all this.

If the guy answered the phone.

chapter 6

With a couple of days off ahead of him, Dan began to think that it might be fun to hike down into the Mokelumne Canyon to see what it was really like. But more important, he was hoping to see Kristen Gallagher, and hoped she felt the same way.

Dan was still surprised that someone as beautiful and nice as Kristen was willing to spend some time with him. That always left him feeling as if he were on the edge of impending disaster. He wanted to spend more time with Kristen but was terrified that she might finally figure out that he wasn't that interesting. And recently, things seemed to be moving sideways, rather than forward with Kristen.

It made for some complicated internal dialogue.

But Dan had an ally in Cal's wife, Maggie. She often included Kristen in her dinner parties, and it was after one of those that Dan and Kristen began to do something that might be considered dating in this day and age. Not that it was easy.

Between Kristen's schedule as a caterer, and Dan's work on many of the weekends, it wasn't easy to find a day when they were both free. And that seemed harder now than it had seemed in the beginning. Dan hoped that wasn't a pattern that was going to get worse.

Still, it was worth a shot.

He called Kristen and was delighted to have her answer the phone immediately.

The last time they had seen each other was nearly ten days ago, although Dan had called twice to leave messages.

"I'm sorry, Dan," Kristen apologized. "I went down to Modesto to help a friend who had a big wedding to do last weekend. But I'm back in town, and would love to see you…"

Once again, Dan was surprised at how easy it was. "Me, too," he said. "I was thinking about a hike… maybe over by Ebbetts Pass…"

Kristen thought this over. "You mean a day-hike? Or did you want to go backpacking?"

"Either one," Dan admitted. He didn't want to give her any reason to turn him down.

"I don't think I could do a backpacking trip," she said. "I don't think I could get away for that long. But Tuesday would work for a day hike… if it's not too long."

"Great!" Dan replied. "We'll work with whatever timing you need."

Kristen laughed—a sound that made Dan grin like a kid on his end. He could listen to that laugh forever. "Okay. How about nine to five?" she said. "How long does it take to drive over there? A couple of hours?"

Dan had to admit he hadn't checked this. But Kristen had lived here longer than he had. She was probably right. "Yeah, about that," he bluffed. "But that should give us a few hours to explore…"

"Sounds like you have a plan in mind," Kristen said.

Dan didn't want to make the date into a research project. He was sure of that. "Not really," he said. "I had a phone call the other day about the Mokelumne Canyon, and I didn't know much about it.

So, I thought we could check it out. Just see what it's like."

"Wow," Kristen sounded surprised. "When you said Ebbetts Pass, I thought you meant something like Nobles Lake or something."

Dan thought he might have detected just a hint of apprehension in her voice.

"We could do that if you'd rather," he said. He could always go back to the canyon on his own.

"No, that's fine," Kristen said. "I haven't been down before. So it will be fun."

To Dan, that last sentence sounded a bit too determined, as if she was going to try to make it fun.

"Well, I don't know how good the trail is down there," he admitted. "We might just hike down a bit and check out the river. There might even be a swimming hole or two."

"That does sound like fun," Kristen agreed. "I'll bring the lunch, and you can bring the swimming toys." She laughed.

"How about a bottle of wine?" Dan asked.

"Mmm, if you want," Kristen said. "But I don't like to drink in the middle of a warm day if I have to hike out later. Maybe save that for a dinner some other time."

Dan agreed with this, since it seemed to imply that dinner another time was expected. "Sure, that's fine."

The conversation paused, as if both were unwilling to bring the call to an end.

Just as Kristen started to say something, Dan said "You know, you don't always have to bring the food. I'm happy to do that sometimes."

"Oh, don't worry," she said. "I've got a kitchen full of odds and ends, and I'll just grab a few things that will work for a hike."

"Okay." Dan agreed. "What were you going to say?" he asked.

"Oh, nothing," Kristen reassured him. "Isn't that where they found the car of that woman who went missing?" Her voice had taken on a quieter, more somber tone.

"I think so," Dan said. "Doris was telling me about that this morning. Apparently, she knew the woman…"

"So did I," Kristen said. "Carol. She hired me a couple of times for her bookstore. She was a really nice lady."

"Yeah, that's what Doris said," Dan replied.

Another silence.

"Okay," Kristen ended it. "So we're set. You bring the pool toys and I'll bring lunch."

"Sounds delicious. I can hardly wait," Dan said. "I'll pick you up at nine."

"Okay," Kristen agreed. "But pick me up at the kitchen. I'll just pack up everything and we can just leave from there."

chapter 7

When Dan pulled up in front of Kristen's kitchen on the day of the hike, the parking lot was empty except for her car. He went up and knocked on the door, peering in through the glass as he did so.

Kristen came out of the back with her arms full of bags, and after she had put them down to open the door, she handed them to Dan.

"This is our lunch?" Dan asked. "You know, we have to carry all of this on the hike."

Kristen smiled. "You're big and strong. And it's not that heavy," she said. "Besides, we can leave some of it in the car for a snack when we get back."

Dan hefted the bags. He guessed something close to ten pounds and wished that he had brought along more than just a small daypack.

But Kristen had packed it all carefully, and she had her own pack as well. By the time they had the food in Dan's car, they were already running late.

"Are you worried about the time?" Kristen asked.

Dan shook his head. He was slightly distracted by the sight of Kristen's slim legs in the seat next to him as he drove. "Nope," he said. "We'll do just fine—we can just follow the trail until we decide it's time to turn around."

Dan enjoyed the drive over to Ebbetts Pass, climbing up

through the small towns on Highway 4, and then shooting up past Bear Valley and Lake Alpine, full of families at this time of year. Then the road really narrowed, and the twists and turns started in earnest.

When they got to the trailhead, Dan packed up his daypack until it was almost bursting with food. Small containers of salads, some fruit, another container of cookies, plus some cheese, some salami, and Dan struggled to find a way to fit in a bottle of water or two in the outside pockets. The poor pack looked ready to explode.

Kristen offered to carry some of the food, but Dan resisted. That's when Kristen saw the sign at the trailhead. Weathered almost to the point of being illegible, it stood above the trail, the letters burned black into the dark wood of the sign.

Kristen read it slowly, sometimes tracing the letters with her fingers to make sure she was reading it correctly.

"The route down canyon is unmaintained and often indefinite. Advance backcountry skills required. The route is not advised for horse travel. Impassable for stock four miles downstream below Monty Wolfe's upper camp. This most wild place deserves our protection and respect. Walk gently and leave no trace."

It was signed the Calaveras Ranger District of the Stanislaus National Forest.

"Wow," she said. "That is the least welcoming sign I have ever seen on a trailhead!"

Dan laughed. "Just trying to keep the riff-raff out," he said. "This isn't really my neck of the woods, but we won't get past those first four miles anyway."

"So we can take our horses?" Kristen laughed.

"I forgot to pack those," Dan said. "They wouldn't have fit in the pack, anyway."

And with that, they shouldered their packs and started down the trail.

For the first mile, Dan was a bit disappointed. The trail followed the canyon but seemed to avoid getting too close to the river. From above they could see deep teal blue pools scattered in among the white granite boulders of the canyon, and occasionally the gentle rush of water came to them above the breezes in the trees. It was beautiful, but Dan wanted to be closer to the river.

The trail here was easy to follow, but it quickly got more complicated as it left the forested hillside to navigate patches of bare granite. Kristen was leading the way, but she drew up short at one section above a series of granite ledges.

"I'm not sure exactly where the trail goes," Kristen confessed, as she waved her hand in front of herself.

Dan walked up to join her. "Well, the good news is that we know where the trail goes," he said. "Somehow, it goes down the canyon. The question is how it gets there."

He pointed to a section of the trail visible in the flatter area far below them. "We just have to get down to that, and we can follow it again."

Kristen slowly picked her way through a section of boulders and granite shelves and was soon down on a recognizable section of the trail again.

"Is that what they mean by an 'indefinite trail?'" she asked.

Dan laughed. "I think it gets a lot more indefinite further down."

After another hour they had reached Deer Creek, which came rushing down from the right and nearly doubled the volume of the river it joined.

Dan caught Kristen looking at her watch.

"Want to stop here?" he asked. "There are some nice falls up above here on the creek. We could check those out."

They had seen no one on the trail, and Dan noted very few footprints in the dust. He led the way up along Deer Creek, picking his way through rough jumbles of boulders. Within a few minutes he was able to show Kristen the waterfall.

"This is lovely," she said.

"And I bet there's nobody here for miles." Dan replied. And noticing a few pangs in his stomach, "Better yet, it feels like lunchtime."

It was more food than they could eat, but Dan forced himself to try everything, from the pickled beets and the cucumber salad to the stuffed grape leaves and the four different cheeses. He was glad Kristen had suggested they leave the wine at home.

After lunch, they tried and failed to look for a way to cross the creek and continue downstream. There was just enough water in the creek to make it dangerous to cross, and Dan didn't see any reason to push the issue, particularly because Kristen was clearly uncomfortable with the idea.

Besides, Kristen's lunch had filled his belly, and he felt the inexorable pull of a nap on his eyelids.

"Time for a rest," Kristen declared, and set off towards a shady grove of pine trees overlooking the spot where the two streams met.

Dan followed her for a hundred yards, and they quickly found a place to sit on a bed of pine needles, with their backs against a fallen tree. There was no sound except the distant rushing of the water and the occasional squawk of a blue jay. A few big black Sierra ants wandered around the pine needles.

He leaned over and gave Kristen a soft kiss.

She smiled, then pushed him gently away. "Not now," she said quietly. "Not down here…" She flicked an ant off her sleeve. "Too many little friends."

Dan looked at her in surprise. She closed her eyes and settled herself in.

Dan gave a look around. Beyond their shady grove, the sunlight streamed through the trees, baking the granite into a white glare where it shined through. He could smell the soft vanilla of the Jeffrey pines and hear the burble of the rushing water below.

He looked back at Kristen, already well on her way to being asleep. He gave a small shrug, and closed his eyes. Within minutes he found himself drifting off to sleep.

He awoke with a start to find that Kristen was nowhere to be seen.

He stood up quickly and looked around him. The stream was still rushing. He could feel the air moving lightly against his cheek. The sun on the granite was just a little too bright for his eyes after his nap, and he held his hand up to shade them.

Even though he was only a few miles from the trailhead, the sense of isolation was profound. He and Kristen were very alone here. The noises of the water only compounded that feeling. Sometimes, when he was completely alone on a river, he was sure he could hear voices in the sounds of the rushing water. He heard those now, and wondered if they really were voices, or just the chuckling river.

He realized he didn't know where Kristen was. He walked back up to the waterfall but didn't see her. He turned around and walked back down to the confluence of the two streams. Dan didn't want to call out, didn't want to sound alarmed. But he couldn't see her anywhere.

"Hello," Kristen's voice came from behind him. Dan turned to look at her.

"Just a quick pit stop," she said, by way of explanation. "Is it about time to start back?"

Dan nodded. "Yeah, I think so…"

As they put on their packs, Kristen turned to look down canyon into the gorge of the Mokelumne. "This is really beautiful," she said.

Dan smiled. "I'm glad you like it."

"But boy, it is certainly quiet out here." Kristen continued. "There is just nobody here at all. It kinda makes you think, doesn't it?"

Dan agreed. The only sounds were the river and a soft breath of wind through the trees. Dan told her about a river where he stood in the canyon and watched an osprey sail down through the trees, following the river. "It's probably too early for one to make an appearance now," he said.

Kristen stared up the canyon for a few minutes. The only sound was the river. "What would you do if you needed help down here?" she asked.

Dan chuckled. "You'd wait a long time," he said. He put his arms around her from behind. "But I don't think we need any help, do we?"

Kristen shook her head, then pulled away from him. "Time to get back to civilization," she said. Then she started walking.

Dan followed her back up the trail, towards the first stretch of granite, and then back out toward the car.

During an easy section of the trail where it wandered along winding route through an open forest, Kristen talked to him over her shoulder.

"Do you ever get nervous out here, being alone?" she asked.

Dan shook his head, even though she couldn't see him. "No. There's really nothing out here to worry about," he said. "The Sierra is wonderful that way. There are no natural predators. We're the top of the food chain."

"But what if you got hurt?" Kristen asked.

"I pay a little more attention to where I'm walking when I'm alone," Dan admitted. "But that's about it."

"What about other people?" she asked.

Dan laughed. "I think you leave most of them behind when you hike about two hundred yards from the trailhead," he said. "Bad guys don't want to work this hard. Besides, they would then have to hike back out again. Too risky for them. If they ever did get up here, they'd rather just break into your car at the trailhead."

"Has that ever happened to you?" Kristen asked.

"No," Dan assured her. "But I don't leave much in it, anyway. So there's not much to take. Still, we don't really have an issue with that around here."

"Breaking into cars?" Kristen made sure she understood.

"Right. I think that happens more at trailheads near cities or towns." He considered her questions again. "Are you worried?" he asked.

"No, not really," she said. "I was just thinking."

So she was worried, at least a little, Dan concluded. "Good," he replied. "This is too beautiful a place to spend much time worrying about things like that."

As they approached the granite jumbles that had confused Kristen on the way down, she stopped again.

"It seems really obvious from this direction," she said.

Dan smiled. "Yeah. That's the way it works, sometimes. Maybe it's because you've done it before."

"No," Kristen corrected him. "It's clearer from this side." She started working her way up through the granite.

They didn't see anyone on the trail out, either.

chapter 8

Once back in Dan's car, they drove back through the twisty one-and-a-half-lane road towards Lake Alpine.

"I always worry I am going to meet someone on this road," Kristen said. "It is so narrow, and people drive so crazy."

Dan slowed down. "There's enough room if people drive slowly—and least in most parts," he said. Just then he had to hit the brakes as a motorcycle came flying around a corner well over on his side of the road. As Dan quickly slammed on the brakes and jerked the truck over to the side of the road, the motorcycle shot past them with a roar.

"Jesus," Dan said. "There's someone who wants to die."

Kristen gave a long and loud sigh. "Thank you for driving," she said. "I'm glad I don't have to do it."

As they finally drove out of the narrow section, back into two lanes near Lake Alpine, Kristen apologized.

"I'm sorry we have to get back," she said.

Dan assured her that he was fine with that.

"I just need to prep some stuff for tomorrow," Kristen explained.

Dan asked her who the client was.

"Well," she began. "You'll think it's crazy, but it's for some guys from E Clampus Vitus."

Dan shot a look over at her. "Really?"

"You know them?" she asked.

"Only by reputation," Dan said. "One of my professors in college was a member of the local chapter up north."

"Yeah, well, I don't think any of these guys are university professors," Kristen said. "They mainly just like to get together and drink. Which they do a lot. Drink, that is."

Dan laughed. "When we first got to that trailhead back there, I thought that sign might have been put there by Clampers," he admitted.

Kristen smiled. "It had a little bit of their sense of humor, didn't it?" she said.

"And it just had that slightly unofficial look to it," Dan added.

"I wonder if those guys put a plaque down at that old campsite on the sign…" Kristen mused.

"Monty Wolfe's? That would be the kind of thing they would do." Dan agreed. "But I'm not sure they'd want to make the trek down there to put it up."

Kristen snorted. "The guys I know wouldn't!"

"So how many people are in the group up here?" Dan asked.

"I'm not sure about all of them," Kristen said. "It seems like there are maybe five or six guys who get together regularly, but I don't know about membership." She thought for a moment. "That seems small, doesn't it? I'm not sure these are all official meetings."

"I don't think there are many rules for that organization," Dan said. "I think each chapter kind of writes its own rules. The one at college was pretty active with the local historical society. They put up lots of plaques and things."

"I've seen some of those plaques," Kristen said. "But I'm not sure the guys who hire me are involved in many of those. At least, I've never seen anything like that. They just want to get together at somebody's house and drink. And eat." She grinned at Dan. "That's where I come in."

"Too bad," Dan laughed. "If they only wanted to drink, we could still be out there…"

Kristen grew quiet.

"Were you hoping to get further down that trail?" she asked.

Dan smiled. "No. That trail goes on for miles and miles. And the farther you go, the worse it gets. I was just happy to check out the falls and get a sense of what it's like down there."

"Not suitable for stock," Kristen added. "That's what the sign says."

"Yeah," Dan agreed. "But from what I've been able to figure out, it gets to the point where there isn't much of a trail at all," he said. "Not suitable for stock; hard to find for humans."

"Are you thinking of going down there again?" Kristen asked.

Dan nodded. "Yeah, maybe take my pack and spend a few days down there, checking things out."

"Well, I'm sorry," Kristen apologized again.

"Don't be," Dan insisted. "We had a great time. The lunch was amazing. I always love hiking with you." He looked over at her. "Didn't you have a good time?"

"Oh yeah," she admitted. "It was nice. Lonely. But nice."

Dan smiled. At the very least, it seemed like Kristen had enjoyed herself.

chapter 9

Back at his house, Dan thought about Kristen. She was a mystery to him.

At first, he had kept Kristen at arm's length. She was wonderful—seemed to bring sunshine into every room she entered. Even now he could smell her—delicate, floral, and completely bewitching. But he was wary. After his divorce, Dan promised himself he'd never put himself into a situation where he could get hurt that badly ever again. He was polite, he was kind... but he wasn't going to fall head over heels in love. Not even with someone as beautiful as Kristen. But when he put his arm around her waist, she floated next to him, danced in the air next to him. At least, that's what it felt like.

But he was being careful, he kept reminding himself.

And she seemed okay with that. He was never really sure why, but she seemed to like him, and give him opportunities to see her again. A movie, a dinner. The dates were always low key. They weren't exactly kids, anyway. They were both taking things slowly, and they both seemed perfectly happy with that. The goodnight kisses had progressed well beyond that stage, but there was still a part of her that Dan didn't seem to know, couldn't seem to reach.

Even when they made love, she was at times distant. Responsive, even passionate. But still a bit distant.

He wondered if he was doing something wrong. He even asked

her about it. She assured him that he was not. It would just take time, she said. She clearly was in no hurry. And Dan respected that. He sensed that if he pushed too hard, he would push her away, maybe forever. And it was becoming clear to Dan that he really didn't want to do that. Not ever.

So much for not falling in love.

But over the last month, Dan had begun to realize that he wanted more. He thought about her more. He wanted to be with her more. It scared the hell out of him, because he worried that those feelings were all on his side. She was often reserved—quick to make an escape if she thought things were getting too serious, or too intimate. He respected that. He had to. After all, she was clearly out of his league. They had to play by her rules.

He just wished he understood the rules better.

He remembered the time that he had greeted her once by saying, "Hi, beautiful." It was as if the sun had suddenly gone behind a cloud. Her face fell and Dan swore that a chill breeze had blown over them.

"Don't call me that," she had said with a catch in her voice. And then, after a short pause, she must have realized that it all sounded odd. "Just call me Kristen," she had told him.

"Okay," he had agreed, easily. An awkward silence had followed.

He tried again. "But I think you are… really lovely," he offered. And then he added, "Kristen."

She smiled. "Thank you," was all she had said. And she had left Dan with far more to think about than when the conversation had begun.

It wasn't something he could talk to Cal about. He'd tried once, and Cal had laughed and told him that if he ever figured it out, he could make millions by writing a book to explain it all to every other man in the world. Which wasn't very helpful to Dan. So Dan had laughed and played along, and promised to sign a copy of the book for Cal.

He'd even thought about talking to Cal's wife Maggie. But if he did that, he was sure it would change their relationship forever. Besides, Maggie was the one who had introduced him to Kristen, and he didn't want to make her feel as if she had to do all the work herself. And afraid that she might just try to do that.

This was his problem, and he would have to solve it. With Kristen's help, of course. That was if he could find a way to ask her. But when they were together, somehow, he never found the way to raise the subject. Or maybe he was just so distracted by the joy of being with her that he didn't want to screw it up by talking about such things.

That was the hard part. And if she didn't want to help, Dan had a much bigger problem.

And on that happy note, he tried to fall asleep.

chapter 10

The next day, Dan drove to Angels Camp to sit in on a meeting of stakeholders in the central Sierra. It was a group that met every six months to raise any issues that went beyond the various jurisdictions that were represented. Dan noted three or four other USFS employees, as well as a couple of different conservation groups. And the guys in the matching golf shirts and baseball caps over there were from a big lumber operation.

Dan wasn't a big fan of these meetings, and he rarely had a topic to raise with the group. But Steve Matson assured him that if someone from the Stanislaus National Forest wasn't at the meeting, they were sure to bring something up that was going to make their life miserable.

Dan had to admit that Steve was probably right. But since Dan was only really going as an observer, he usually took along something to read. He wasn't obvious about it. He didn't bring a stack of magazines. But he did bring along a nice folder of official reports that he was supposed to have read by now. And by the end of the meeting, he expected he would be up to date on those.

As they gathered outside the restaurant where they were to meet, Dan noticed another pale green pickup drive up. It was probably from the Eldorado Forest, he guessed.

A short but fit young man hopped out of the truck, and Dan

noticed a long blond ponytail when the driver turned to lock the truck.

"You don't think anyone is actually interested in stealing that thing, do you?" he called out with a grin.

The young man looked up and chuckled. "Hey, just following the rules," he said. Peering at Dan's name tag, he held out his hand and said, "Chris Martin."

Dan shook his hand and introduced himself. "Are you from Eldorado?" he asked.

Chris nodded, looking around at the rest of the group.

"What's your role there?" Dan asked.

"I'm the wilderness ranger," Chris answered with a laugh. "Can't you tell?"

"What are you doing here?" Dan asked. It wasn't the usual sort of duty for someone like Chris.

Chris looked around again, leaned toward Dan, and said, conspiratorially, "Pretty wild bunch here. They figured I was the best match."

Dan laughed. Despite his small stature, Chris stood with his shoulders back and his neck straight, and it gave him the look of someone who was ready for action. Dan decided he liked the look.

"I was over on your side of the forest yesterday," Dan said.

Chris asked him where he had been.

"Hermit Valley. Hiking down into the Mokelumne," Dan answered.

Chris looked at him with new interest. "How far did you get? Did you get past Deer Creek?'

Dan shook his head. "Water was a little high," he said. "And I was with someone who didn't like the way it looked." To protect his male vanity Dan didn't want Chris to think he had stopped on his own.

"It's pretty wild down there," Chris told him. "I'd like to do some trail work down there, but it's hard to convince anyone of the priority of that. Not when we have Carson Pass and Silver Lake to manage."

Dan told him about his conversation with Steve Matson. "Seems like both sides of the coin have the same plan," he said. "Do nothing, and hope nobody goes down there."

"Well, I've been down there," Chris said. "It's not that bad. At least, not the part that I saw. There is a trail, of sorts, but it hasn't been maintained for God knows how many years."

Dan asked him how far he had hiked into the canyon.

"From Hermit Valley, only a few miles," Chris admitted. "But we have a couple of other trails that go down there…"

Just then the group was called into the restaurant to start the meeting. Dan led the way, and was hoping to continue the conversation, but Chris saw someone else he knew, and stopped to say hello.

Dan ended up sitting at the far end of the table from the Chair, and he managed to read all the reports that he had brought along. In fact, he read them in the first hour and a half. Which meant he had another hour and a half of meeting to go.

It was a long ninety minutes. But the end finally came.

As he was standing up, Chris came back over to Dan and walked out to his truck with him.

"If you're interested in the Mokelumne, I've got some crews going in there in the next couple of weeks," he said. "I don't know what your situation is, but you're welcome to join us."

Dan told him about Steve Matson's directive: not on company time.

Chris laughed. "Yeah, I've heard that line too many times," he said. "But if you're interested, I have a group going in this weekend. Volunteers. I don't know how many will show up, but we can use all the help we can get. Going in either Saturday or Sunday, and trying to put in a full day down there."

Dan asked him for details. As he took in the information, Dan ran through his own schedule in his mind. He seemed to remember that he had this coming weekend off.

Or, as Steve would say, not on company time.

"You know what?" Dan said. "I think that could work." He exchanged cards with Chris and offered to bring a few tools that might be needed.

"Don't worry about that," Chris said. "I'll have everything we need. All we need is the people to use 'em."

"Cool," Dan said. "I'll be one of the people."

chapter 11

When Dan drove up to the trailhead to join the work crew, he didn't see Chris or his truck. There were a couple of women that he guessed were in their fifties sitting in a bright blue Subaru wagon, and Dan walked over to say hello.

"Are you waiting for Chris Martin?" he asked them.

The women hesitated for a moment before answering. "Is he the ranger?" they asked.

Dan nodded.

"I guess that's who we're waiting for," the woman on the passenger's side of the car told him. "We were just told to be here at 8:30…"

The driver leaned over towards Dan and added: "We've really never done this before, so we're not sure quite what we're doing."

Dan smiled. "How did you hear about this?" he asked.

"We're in the Native Plant Society, and someone mentioned it at our last meeting." The passenger said. "I'm Pat."

"And I'm Janet," the driver added.

"Nice to meet you," Dan said. "I'm Dan."

"Have you done one of these before, Dan?" Janet asked him.

Dan admitted that he had done quite a few. But not in the Eldorado Forest.

Of course, they wanted to know where, and Dan explained that he was a ranger based in the Stanislaus Forest. "You're actually in the Stanislaus National Forest right here," he said. "But once we start heading down into the canyon, we'll be in the Eldorado."

"Is this something like a joint venture?" Janet asked. "You guys working together?"

Dan shook his head. "Nope, this is all Chris. I'm just here as a volunteer, like you."

The two women told Dan that they thought it was really generous of him to help out on his day off. "You're not the typical government employee," Pat told him.

Dan laughed. "I've been told that before," he said. He was about to add more when he saw Chris drive into the parking lot. The truck pulled up right next to Janet's car, and Chris waved.

"Good to see you have introduced yourselves," he said to Dan.

"Oh yeah, we're old friends now," Dan said.

Chris got out of his truck and started pulling tools out of the back: a shovel, a few pairs of loppers, a McLeod, a small hand saw.

He stared into the truck bed. "Do you think we'll need the big buck saw?" he asked Dan.

Dan shrugged. "Not down to Deer Creek." Dan answered. "There were only a couple of small trees across the trail. We can do them easily with the hand saw."

Chris turned and looked up at the sky. "It is going to be really hot today," he said.

Janet agreed. "Don't worry," she said. "We brought lots of water."

Chris looked back to look in the truck bed, then turned to Dan. "You didn't make it across the creek, did you?"

Dan shook his head. "No…"

"I'm thinking that we might find a tree to drop across the

creek," Chris continued, as he pulled the big saw out of the truck.

Chris handed out tools to the rest of the group. Pat and Janet each got a pair of loppers, and Dan carried a shovel and a McCleod. Chris took the big saw and strapped it on his pack. He picked up a mattock in one hand and led the way down the trail.

Pat and Janet were suitably impressed by the warning sign at the trailhead, but Dan assured them that the first few miles would be fine.

As they hiked down the trail, Chris pointed out areas that needed cutting back with the loppers. "But we'll leave that to do on our way out," he said. "I'd rather take care of some of the stuff farther down, first."

They stopped at the first big granite section that had baffled Kristen. Chris and Dan discussed how to route the trail through the rocks and ledges, while the two women began to get bored.

"We'll go ahead and start lopping down there," Janet said, pointing to a section of the trail that was being overgrown with whitethorn and huckleberry oak.

"Great!" Chris told them. "Just remember, you're not trimming a hedge in the garden. Cut it way back as far as you can, down by the roots. I don't want to have to come back in a year or two and do this all over again."

Pat assured him that they would be "brutal," and Chris laughed. "Good. This isn't a topiary!"

Then he turned to Dan, and the two of them stared at the granite.

"The right thing to do would be to move that big boulder to serve as a step," Chris said.

Dan looked at the rock. "I'm guessing that rock is just a hair short of too big to move," he said. "Let's make sure we don't have to move it twice."

Forty-five minutes later, the two men stood back to check out their work. "It's not perfect," Chris said.

"It's a hell of a lot better than it was," Dan assured him. "And at least the trail is clear now. You won't have people wandering all over this." He waved at the granite.

"That's still a big step down at the bottom," Chris complained.

"Not recommended for stock," Dan reminded him with a grin.

"Yeah, okay," Chris agreed. "I guess we can always come back and work on it later. Let's see how Pat and Janet are doing."

The two men didn't catch up to Pat and Janet until the trail hit Deer Creek.

"You guys got a lot done," Chris enthused.

Janet laughed. "I told Pat that we could stop for lunch when we got to the creek. That was all the incentive we needed."

Chris checked his watch. "Yeah, I guess it is lunchtime." He turned to Dan. "This good?"

Dan noticed the fallen tree that he had leaned against only a few days ago. "I know it well. Works perfectly for lunch."

Dan was grateful for the shade. He pulled out his sandwich and took a bite. He was coming to the conclusion that working with Chris was fun. They had a similar approach to problem solving, and Dan had to admit that Chris' rate of work was even greater than his own. He'd had to push a little to keep up with the smaller man. They got a lot done together.

Janet and Pat had started on their lunches and were now engaged in questioning Dan about his work, his life, and, well, just about everything. When their questions slowed down, Dan noted that Chris had disappeared. He finished up his lunch and started packing things away.

Pat was complaining about the heat, and Dan asked her if she needed more water.

"It's just working out in that sun," Pat said. "We need to find a section of the trail that needs work in the shade."

"Why don't you work on routing the trail through here?" Dan heard Chris say from behind him. "It kind of just disappears when it gets near the creek, and it would be good to show where it goes now."

"Where does it go now?" Janet asked. "I thought this was where it ends."

Chris pointed to a tall lodgepole pine snag behind him. "See that tree? I think we can drop that across the creek and get to the trail on the other side."

He looked at Dan, who stood up. "Sounds like it's time to get back to work," he said.

The two men walked over to the creek and sized up the tree. As they stared at the tree, and the creek, Chris slowly pointed with his arm, showing where he hoped the tree would fall.

Dan nodded. It would be a warm afternoon's work.

chapter 12

Between cutting the wedges, clearing a few smaller trees, and making enough room for them to work around it, it took them most of an hour to drop the tree across the creek. As the saw bit through and the trunk began to crack, Dan raced off to one side, while Chris ran off in the other direction. Being close to a falling tree was a great way to get injured, and both men knew it.

When Dan turned to look at the fallen tree, it had landed almost perfectly where they wanted it. He joined Chris by the stump to admire their work. "That was just about perfect," he said.

Chris made a wry face. "I'd like to see if we can move that far end to go upstream of that big rock," he said, pointing across. "That way it might not get washed down in the spring."

Dan thought this over. He knew Chris was right, but it would take a huge amount of effort to move the log now. He watched as Chris gingerly climbed up on the trunk and started to ease himself across the creek. When he got to the middle of the trunk, Chris gave a couple of small bounces on it. "Seems pretty solid," he called out to Dan.

Dan watched as Chris continued across, then climbed up on the log himself. It was just a bit narrower than he would have liked, but he had crossed many a creek on logs smaller than this.

"I think it's great," he told Chris. "It's going to make a big difference."

When he had joined Chris on the far side of the creek, Dan realized that he was back in the sun, and it was beating down on him.

Chris was considering the tree in front of him. "You know, I knew we should have brought that rock bar," he said. "A little leverage right now would be a big help."

Dan thought about how far away the truck was—too far for today. He walked off up the hill, looking for a large branch to use. The only ones he found were either too small to work, or too old and brittle.

Chris called out from behind him. "I think we can try this one," he said. He was holding a curved branch that just might work, if they could turn it the right direction.

They wedged the fat end of the branch under the tree and gave a heave. With a crack, the branch broke off in their hands. It was now only about five feet long.

"Not a lot of leverage there now," Dan said.

Chris handed Dan the end of the branch. "Why don't you try to keep using this, and I'll get down there and try to push from below."

Dan took a grip on the branch and wedged it tightly under the tree. "Be careful down there," he said to Chris. "I'm going to try not to drop the whole tree on you."

"I appreciate that," Chris said. "You ready?"

Dan nodded. When he saw Chris push, Dan gave a heave on the branch. The tree shuddered and then started to move, slowly up the side of the rock.

"It's moving!" he called to Chris. "But I'm about out of branch here."

"Can you hold it?" Chris asked.

"I think so," Dan said.

Chris quickly hopped away from the tree and came back to Dan with a large rock. With a grunt he heaved the rock under the tree, and Dan let up.

Using a series of rocks and levers, the two men slowly worked the tree up to the top of the large boulder in stages, and then eased it over the other side. It slid down into place with a crashing thump.

They stood on the side of the creek admiring their work.

"Nice bridge," Dan said.

Chris nodded. "It should work."

Dan pulled out his phone and took a photo. "Want a picture?" he asked Chris.

"Hell, no," Chris said. "I'm not even supposed to be down here."

Dan gave him a confused look.

"If my boss knew I was down here working on this trail today, he'd be pissed," Chris explained. "This is very definitely not a priority."

"Got it," Dan said, putting away his phone. "No photos."

Chris sat down next to Dan and pulled out a bottle of water. "If those women weren't here, I might just jump in," he said, staring at the water.

Dan chuckled. "I'm not sure they'd care," he said. "But I know what you mean. It is damn hot."

Chris sat back and gave a huge sigh. "Seems like every time I get down into this canyon, it's hot," he said. "Or something happens…"

Dan shot him a curious glance.

Chris shook his head. "The craziest trail crew ever," he said. "It was a group of volunteers from all over the place, organized by some hiking group online. Some of them flew in from the East Coast. There was even a guy from China. It was the only way I could get approval to work in this canyon. I had to explain to my boss that they had all come in just to work here."

Dan smiled. He understood the ways and means of working with the government.

"And so the thing has been set up for months. And it's smoky as hell from all the fires last summer. Not great conditions. The first day, we hike in about two miles, and before we can even stop for lunch, one of the women slips on the trail and breaks her leg."

Dan looked at Chris. "Not ideal," he said.

"Sub-optimal," Chris agreed. "I've got a pack train headed down into the canyon with all of our supplies, and the packer won't leave the stuff unless I'm there. But somehow, I have to get this woman back to the trailhead. "

"With a broken leg," Dan reminded him.

"Yeah, well, we weren't sure it was broken," Chris clarified, "But she could barely stand up. I mean, she couldn't keep hiking… let alone with a pack on."

"What did you do?" Dan asked.

"I had one guy on the trip that I knew from before, and he was pretty solid. So I decided that he should try to help her back out to the trailhead, and the rest of us would keep going. I mean, I had to be there, because I was the only one who knew where the camp was. It was either that or call off the whole trip and send the whole group home."

Dan nodded. "With the pack train. And with all those people who were expecting to get to work."

"Right. But just as I was about to explain that to everybody, that guy I knew started running like hell down the trail. And a few seconds later I heard a motor, and he managed to flag down a couple of guys in a jeep who were driving around back there."

"There was a road?" Dan asked.

"Not exactly. It's an abandoned four-wheel drive track, and these guys were not really supposed to be there," Chris said. "But I wasn't going to bitch at that point. I was just happy to see them."

"Yeah, no kidding," Dan agreed.

"Here's the funny part. They had driven back there so that they could hike down into the canyon. They were on their way out when we saw them. And they were a complete mess. They were scratched up and bleeding; their clothes were torn. One guy really only had part of a boot left on his foot. So they made it down into the canyon, and back out again, but they swore they would never do that again."

Dan chuckled. "Down to hell and back," he said.

Chris nodded. "I only talked to them for a couple of minutes, but it didn't sound like they'd had much fun. They said there were miles of brush to whack through. One guy swore that he had heard a pair of mountain lions screaming at each other."

"Wow," Dan said. Even in his years as a wilderness ranger, that was something he had never heard.

"They had some stories to tell," Chris continued. "And I don't think they were all that happy about the trip. They even said the fishing was poor."

"Which is what every fisherman says about their secret spot," Dan suggested.

Chris laughed. "Yeah, true enough."

"Give them three months," Dan said, "and it will have been a great adventure. They'll tell the story for the rest of their lives."

"Yeah, maybe," Chris agreed. "At least once the scars had grown over."

Pat and Janet appeared on the far side of the creek and waved.

"We thought you guys were working hard." Janet complained. "But you're just sitting there in the shade."

Chris laughed and pointed to the new log bridge.

Janet examined it. "Nice," she said, although she didn't look as if she wanted to cross it. "We are going to start back out. Maybe we'll lop some of that brush on the way out."

Chris nodded. "That's fine. Thank you for the help," he said. "We won't be far behind you."

As the two women hiked back up the trail, Chris asked Dan if he wanted to check out the canyon a bit more. "There's a nice view down here about half a mile," he said.

chapter 13

Chris led the way through a brief section of forest, and then out onto a large granite knob. After some route finding around on the granite, the two men scrambled up the last few feet to the top of the knob. Below them the canyon opened up with a view that went on for many miles.

"Wow," Dan said. "This is really impressive,"

Dan's eyes wandered across the landscape.. On the right, steep granite cliffs towered a thousand or more feet above the canyon. To the left the slopes were only slightly less steep, enough to allow a thick forest of trees to cover most of the rock. But in the floor of the canyon it was all rock: clumps and knobs of granite, colored black by the lichen that had stained it. The river was invisible, even though they could hear it. It lay below them, coursing through the narrow channels and around the ledges and boulders in the bottom.

Chris stood next to him, giving Dan time to take it all in. "My guess is that there isn't another person in that whole canyon down there," he said. "Just granite, some trees, and a river running through it down there somewhere."

"Mainly granite," Dan said. Miles away to the west, Dan could see the canyon take a turn to the left. "Is that where Summit City comes in?" he asked.

Chris nodded. "Yeah. That's another trail that peters out down into here. Part of the old Tahoe Yosemite Trail."

Dan looked up to his right. There was a thin ribbon of white water cascading down from a valley high above the cliffs.

Chris followed his gaze. "You wouldn't want to try that route," he said. "There are a couple of tiny lakes up there, but I think the only way to get to them is from the other side."

As Dan's eyes searched for a route up the cliff, he had to admit it looked like more of an adventure than he was willing to tackle. "Have you been up there?" he asked Chris.

"Only from the other side," Chris said. "It's no cakewalk from that side, either. The lakes sit in a little bowl, and it's a bit of a bushwhack to get down to them from one of the reservoirs up by Blue Lakes."

Dan imagined what Chris meant when he said "a bit of a bushwhack," and smiled. "Nice place to get away from it all?" he suggested.

"You would think," Chris agreed. "But I had a really weird experience up there a couple of years ago."

Dan turned to look at Chris, who was still staring up at the cliff.

Chris turned and met his gaze. "Really strange," he said. "I'll tell you the story on the way back."

Chris motioned for Dan to go first and fell into step behind him. "I was up there for a couple of days," Dan heard him say. "I took the trail from Blue Lakes, and then just spent some time checking out that whole area. But when I hiked down into that bowl, things got really bizarre."

Dan, walking ahead, wanted to stop and ask questions, but he knew they should keep walking. And Chris kept talking.

"As I got down close to the first lake, I was walking along, miles from anyone, and right there in the middle of the forest was a sneaker."

"Somebody lost their shoe?" Dan asked. "It's hard to hike like that. And a sneaker, not a boot?"

Chris grunted. "Maybe a trailrunner. But this was miles from any trailhead. I left it there, figuring that I would pick it up on the way back out," he said. "And about a hundred feet farther down towards the lake, there was another one."

Dan chuckled. "That doesn't sound like fun," he said. "Hiking barefoot. But maybe the guy was hiking in boots, and just got tired of carrying them?"

"I know, right?" Chris replied. "But then I found a shirt. And a sock. It was really weird. By the time I got to the lake, I had found just about a complete set of hiking clothes."

"Man or woman?" Dan asked with a grin. "Just curious."

"Male," Chris answered. He didn't sound amused. "And when I got to the lake, there was a complete campsite: tent, sleeping bag, stove, everything. It was scattered all over the place, and the tent and sleeping bag had been torn to pieces by the animals."

"So, somebody just left it all there?" Dan said. "How did they get out, without shoes?"

"I have no idea," Chris said. "The stuff had been there long enough to be torn up by the wildlife, but it just looked like someone had hiked in there, decided that backpacking wasn't for them, and then hiked back out and just left it all there. Only from that lake, it's probably a good ten or twelve miles to the trailhead. Without shoes. And not really a trail."

"Maybe the sneakers were his camp shoes, and he still had his boots," Dan suggested.

"Maybe," Chris conceded. "It's still a long way with no gear."

Dan thought this over. "Or something happened to him?" he

suggested. "Did you check for a missing person report?"

"Yeah," Chris replied. "At first I was pretty freaked out about it. I reported it, and we did a pretty careful check. No missing person reported. Just a completely abandoned campsite. And it's too bad I got there too late. Some of that gear was nice—top quality stuff."

"Not the kind of stuff that people would normally leave behind," Dan said.

"Exactly," Chris agreed. "And it was only one person. One-man tent, one sleeping bag."

Dan thought this over. "And no serial killers on the loose in the area?" he asked, half joking.

"Yeah," Chris replied. "I thought of that too. But there was nobody missing. They were looking for that guy who killed a bunch of people over in Ukiah then, but that's a long way away…"

"Donald Lamar Graham?" Dan remembered.

"Is that the guy?" Chris said. "Killed his girlfriend and her family, then took off…"

"Yeah. Remember that he was supposed to be this great outdoorsman?" Dan asked. "And then they found out that for a few days he had been living out of a dumpster behind a Walmart."

"Well, don't underestimate the skills you need to do that," Chris grinned.

"Did they ever find him?" Dan asked.

"Who? Graham?" Chris said. "I don't know, I think they decided he'd run off to Canada or something…"

"Well, if nobody was missing…" Dan continued, "it's hard to pin that on a guy living in a dumpster in Canada."

"Exactly," Chris said. After another pause, he repeated, "It was top quality stuff."

"Did you keep any of it?" Dan asked.

"Most of it was trashed—the tent and sleeping bag and all," Chris replied. "A real pain in the ass to drag it all out of there. I think I kept the stove somewhere. Or maybe I donated it to the local scouts or something."

By this time, they were back at the log bridge, and took turns climbing up and over it.

"That works," Chris said with some satisfaction.

"Oh, my god," Dan said. "Check this out."

Ahead of him, Pat and Janet had laid out a complete line of rocks on both sides of the trail for a good quarter of a mile. Every ten to twelve feet they had added a cairn. "It looks like somebody had a lot of time on their hands."

Chris laughed. "Well, at least we won't have to worry about people getting lost down here. Nobody can miss that!"

At the end of the rock walls, Dan stopped to look back at them. "Are you okay with this?" he asked. "It's not exactly how we'd do it," he added sarcastically.

"Volunteers," Chris answered. "They do what they can, how they can. And no, it's not the way I would have done it. But it's done, and it's time to get back to the truck."

Dan nodded. For a wilderness trail, this was clearly overkill. But it wasn't worth undoing the work the women had done. He turned, and this time he followed Chris up the trail.

chapter 14

"So, what happens lower down in the canyon?" Dan asked Chris.

"You mean below Summit City?" Chris asked. "There are some trails that go down there, but none of them connect with each other."

Dan told Chris about Cal's adventure years ago.

"Yeah, that sounds about right," Chris said. "That trail that goes down toward Camp Irene. It meets up with the trail that comes down from our side, but somehow you have to get across the river."

Dan asked Chris if he had ever made it down that far.

"I got down there once last year," Chris replied. "But I did it from our side, not yours. The top part of the trail was fine, but the section that goes straight down into the canyon was just a solid mess of impenetrable brush. But once you get down there, Camp Irene is beautiful."

"Who was Irene?" Dan asked him.

"I'm not sure," Chris admitted. "One of the volunteers told me a story once, but I'm not sure it's true."

"The best stories aren't," Dan suggested, with a smile.

Chris laughed. "Yeah, this guy was one of those Clampers. You know about them?"

Dan grunted to show that he did.

"So the way he told it, there was a wealthy guy in Stockton, or Modesto, somewhere out in the valley, and he bought a whole section of the river as a kind of summer camp, or fishing camp. He'd bring his wife up here, and they'd camp and hang out. He loved to fish…"

"Was this national forest, then?" Dan asked.

"I don't know," Chris said. "This was a long time ago, but I'm not sure when. I'm not sure the guy owned the place, or just used it and nobody ever bothered him about it."

"Another Monty Wolfe, huh?" Dan asked.

Chris stopped and looked at Dan. "What do you know about Monty Wolfe?" He wasn't smiling.

Dan stopped and held his left hand up in mock surrender. "Only what I read on the internet in the last few days," he said. "And I'm not sure how much of that is true."

"You got that right," Chris agreed. He turned back to the trail and started hiking again. "Anyway, that's who started Camp Irene. This guy from Stockton, or wherever."

"And Irene was his wife?" Dan asked.

"Yep," Chris continued. "Only the story I heard, one day the guy went off fishing, and when he came back, Irene was gone."

"You mean she left him?" Dan asked. He could see Chris shaking his head in front of him.

"No, she didn't leave him." Chris said. "But she wasn't in camp. Nowhere to be found."

The two men hiked along for a while, each unwilling to take a break, but each one feeling the exertion enough that talking was an effort.

Finally, Dan called a halt, at the top of the granite wall.

A group of hikers was coming down the trail. To Dan, it looked like a family outing—a mom, dad, a couple of kids, and maybe that older man was grandpa.

Chris stopped and chatted with the hikers. They were just out for the afternoon and wanted to know how much farther it was down to the waterfall.

Chris told them it was about a mile down the trail.

"That's not too bad," said the man. "What, maybe half an hour of hiking?"

Chris smiled and said, "It all depends on how fast you hike."

That's when the grandfather noticed the tools the two rangers were carrying. "Are you guys the ones who maintain this trail?" he asked.

"When we get some time to do it," Dan answered.

"Well, you do a crappy job," the man grumbled. "We heard this trail was getting better, but it's a mess."

"Actually," Chris chimed in, "we're here on our day off, just trying to clean it up a bit."

"Well you need to do a lot more!" the man continued. "What the hell do we taxpayers pay you for?"

"Dad," the wife of the family broke in gently, "they're doing what they can."

"And it's not enough! This trail is in terrible shape!"

Chris gave them a dismissive wave and started up the hill towards the trailhead. Dan wasn't going to give in so easily.

"You do realize that we're working down here on our own time, right?" he asked. "And we are always looking for volunteers. We don't have enough budget to get everything done, and we always welcome anyone who comes out to help us."

"Ha!" the old man grouched. "If you did your job right you wouldn't need help."

"Dad!" The woman was now yelling at her father as loudly as

he was yelling at Dan. "They are here on their day off. You should be thanking them. They are trying to try to fix the trail."

The old man paused his rant and glowered at Dan, then muttered something under his breath and turned away.

"Come on, kids," said the man Dan had identified as the father. "Let's get down to the river and the waterfall."

Dan smiled at the kids. "Have a good time down there, and be safe."

"Thank you," the kids chorused politely.

Dan's eyes locked with the woman's for a moment. She smiled at him, pointed to his shovel, and silently mouthed the words "Thank you" to him.

He gave her a wink and then turned up the trail. He would have to pick up the pace if he wanted to catch Chris.

It was on the last, steep section of the trail that he finally caught up with his friend.

"Did they ever find her?" he asked, between gasping breaths.

Chris stopped hiking and turned around. "Irene?" he said. "Yeah, finally. I guess it was a year or two later. They found her body trapped under a boulder in the river. She must have fallen in and got trapped."

"Oof," Dan exhaled. "Can you imagine running around, not finding her… for hours. For days…"

Chris nodded. "Yeah, I've done enough Search and Rescue to know how people get."

"So did the guy keep coming up here to camp, or what?" Dan asked.

"I don't know," Chris admitted. "But that's the story behind Camp Irene, at least the way I heard it."

"And they didn't find her until the next year?" Dan asked.

"Can you imagine?" Chris asked, over his shoulder, as he started up the trail again, leaving Dan to ponder the fate of Irene, and stare at the buck saw hanging off the back of Chris's pack.

chapter 15

That night Dan logged onto his computer and spent another hour or two looking for stories about Monty Wolfe and Camp Irene. But what he found left him dissatisfied. He had hoped for more specifics, but what little he found was as much rumor as it was history.

His mind wandered back to his college professor, and the next destination for Dan's computer was E Clampus Vitus. He quickly found the local "Matuca" chapter's website, and he began to explore.

Dan's professor had made the organization seem like an ideal combination of good fun and appreciation for local history, and Dan was intrigued. The website included some basic information about the organization, founded during the Gold Rush as a satire of the many other fraternal organizations and their elaborate rituals and ceremonial titles. He chuckled at the title of Grand Noble Humbug who led the local chapter, and even perused the application form, full of jokes, silly tests, and ridiculous songs.

He had just about made up his mind to track down someone in the organization and apply for membership when he read the bylaws that limited membership to men only.

"Really?" he found himself thinking. "In 2022?" And then he began to imagine the initiation ritual. And how the group might respond if he suggested that maybe it was time to include women in the membership. And he clicked away from the application form.

Not his kind of people, in the end, he decided.

But he wondered if they might know more about Monty Wolfe, or if they had ever considered putting up one of their memorial plaques in his memory. He used the website's contact form to leave a question about Monty Wolfe and included his contact information.

It was about then that his phone rang.

Dan was delighted to see it was Chris Martin.

"Just wanted to thank you again for all the help," Chris said. "I'm really happy with what we got done, and that tree should work great as a bridge."

"I had fun," Dan assured him. "Let me know when you're going back in there, and I'll join you if I can."

Chris mentioned a date a couple of weeks ahead, and Dan noted it quickly on his calendar.

Then he took a breath, and asked Chris, "Hey, what's the deal with Monty Wolfe and his cabin?"

There was a short silence as Chris thought this over.

"You know about the cabin, and the preservation guys?" he asked Dan.

Dan told him what he knew. "Is there more to the story?"

"Not really," Chris said. "That cabin is in a very inaccessible part of the canyon. If the cabin weren't there, nobody would go there. But because it's there, people try to go find it. So it's kind of a—what do insurance companies call swimming pools? An attractive nuisance."

Dan asked if Chris had been to the cabin.

"Yeah," Chris sounded unimpressed. "It's down there. It's impressive when you think about one guy building it on his own. But it's also decaying. It won't last forever. I certainly don't think that we ought to try and restore it or repair it."

"Arrested decay," Dan quoted from the Forest Service manual.

"Yeah, I think that's fair," Chris agreed. "But the guy was pretty impressive. Lived off the land in there, except for a few supplies that he'd carry in at the beginning of winter. And there's not that much food down there, as you know."

"He must have lived on fish, a few squirrels, a deer…" Dan suggested.

Chris chuckled. "Nobody ever described him as fat."

As the conversation continued, Dan asked Chris about E Clampus Vitus. "Do you know anything about those guys up here?" he asked. "Ever worked with them?"

Chris laughed. "They tend to march to their own drummer," he said. "I don't think they're much into trail work or anything. Mainly just putting up their brass plaques and having parties."

Dan told Chris about his professor's interest in local history.

"Yeah," Chris said. "There's usually at least one of those guys who has an interest in that sort of thing. But I don't know who it is right now. That's not really my side of things. I'm on the wilderness side, not the cultural and historic artifacts side…"

Dan pulled the website up again on his computer. Under the title of Grand Noble Historian, the website said, "Apply within."

He told Chris it looked like that position was open.

Chris laughed and told Dan to apply.

"No, thanks," Dan said. "I have enough stuff to do, and if I have any free time, I want to spend it in the wilderness, not around a table. Or a bar."

By the end of the conversation, they had agreed to meet in ten days' time at the Hermit Valley trailhead. And this time, it would be a longer trip, both in miles and in days.

This time, they would get down into the gorge itself.

chapter 16

It was a slow day in the Summit Ranger Station, and Dan was behind the counter while Doris took a short break. With the madness of Memorial Day behind them, it would be relatively calm for a few weeks before the summer crowds really hit.

So Dan noticed when a beat up old International Harvester Scout sputtered and clattered into the parking lot. Dan hadn't seen one of those since he visited his grandfather's farm many years before.

The Scout parked in front of the restrooms, where it was hidden from Dan's view. But minutes later he watched a figure walk in front of the windows and open the door.

The man matched his vehicle. Dan guessed that he was well past sixty, with his full gray hair swept back underneath a battered straw cowboy hat. The man wasn't quite six feet tall, but probably weighed enough to compensate for that lack of height. Dan guessed at least 250 pounds, a significant amount of which was concentrated in a large belly hanging over his belt buckle. A thinning handlebar mustache ornamented the suntanned face. His outfit consisted of a truly disreputable pair of jeans, shapeless boots the color of the dirt that covered them, and a denim vest over a stained cowboy shirt, complete with the mother-of-pearl buttons.

Dan looked up and greeted the man with a smile.

"You Dan Courtwright?" the man asked.

"Guilty as charged," Dan admitted.

The man shot his hand out to Dan. "Hoss Adams," he said. "Just call me 'Hoss.'"

Dan nodded. He decided that he wouldn't call the man any name at all unless it was necessary.

Hoss looked at him. "You interested in the Clampers?" he asked Dan.

Dan smiled. "Sure," he said. "I had a professor in college who was a Clamper."

"You left a message on the website," Hoss continued. "That's why I'm here. Well, that and the fact that I've got some horses up by Eagle Meadows that needed some tending, and I figured I'd kill two birds…"

Dan nodded. "Yeah, I left a message about Monty Wolfe. I was wondering if the Clampers ever put up a plaque to him or anything."

Hoss considered this for a minute.

"You know, we probably should," he agreed. "But right now we're a little short-handed in that department." He gave a sigh and stood staring pensively at the counter in front of Dan.

"It just seemed to me that he was the kind of guy that would appeal to your group," Dan suggested.

"Oh yes, I won't dispute that," Hoss agreed. "Are you interested in becoming a member?" he asked Dan.

"I've thought about it," Dan replied. "I'm not sure exactly what's involved."

"Well, you need somebody to sponsor you," Hoss explained. "But I could do that, no problemo. And then you come to a meeting and get initiated." He stopped and looked at Dan. "Bring an extra set of clothes, and don't wear any jewelry or anything. And whatever you do, don't wear anything red. Not even a tiny patch on a sock." He fixed Dan with a stare to make sure that Dan understood this last part.

"Okay," Dan agreed with a nod. "I'll keep that in mind. Things are pretty busy around here, but let me think it over."

Hoss pulled out his wallet and handed Dan his business card. Dan was surprised to see the name of a major local construction company on the card, as well as the man's title. And the card clearly stated that the man's name was, in fact, Hoss.

Dan shook Hoss' hand and thanked him for coming in.

"You'll love the meetings," Hoss said. "There's always way too much to drink, and it's a great bunch of guys."

"Would any of them know more about Monty Wolfe's cabin?" Dan asked.

Hoss thought this over. "You know what you should do? You should come to our next meeting. You can ask the whole group about that. I'll bet there's someone who does." He paused. "Just don't wear anything red…"

Dan chuckled. "Got it. We tend towards earth tones around here anyway," he said.

Hoss looked down at his own clothes. "Well," he said. "I guess if you work with animals, you end up with earth tones no matter what you put on in the morning." He grinned.

Dan couldn't help smiling as Hoss turned and walked towards the door. "Let me know!" Hoss called out over his shoulder as he strode out into the sunlight.

And that's just when Doris walked in the door.

chapter 17

She was not happy.

"I don't think this is at all funny," she said.

Dan looked at her in confusion.

"Unless I am very much mistaken," Doris continued. "That is Carol Lawlor's car in the parking lot." She pointed an accusing finger to a gray Camry on the far side of the lot, far from the ranger station.

Dan gave her a surprised look and a shrug. "I didn't see that," he said. "I don't think it was there when I drove in this morning." He usually noticed what cars were in the parking lot because it gave him an idea of how many permits he was going to be writing in his first few minutes in the office.

"I know it wasn't there," Doris answered hotly. "Because I didn't see it." She stared out at the car through the dusty windows of the ranger station.

Dan looked perplexed.

"I don't think it was there when I went on break," Doris continued. "I'm sure it wasn't."

She shot an accusatory look at Dan.

"I'm sorry, but I had a visitor while you were out," he said. "It was somebody from the Clampers, Hoss Adams." He paused, giving Doris a chance to offer her opinion. Which she did.

"Hmmph," she grunted. "What did he want?" She didn't sound happy.

Dan explained the reasons behind Adams' visit.

"Bunch of old men with nothing better to do," Doris grumped. "If they wanted to help, they could volunteer up here."

It was not like Doris to be so grumpy. Dan wondered if her mood had to do with her memories of Carol Lawlor. That had seemed to be a sensitive subject when Cal mentioned it.

"How well did you know Carol Lawlor?" he asked. Dan was not usually so direct, but after working with Doris for four years, he let some of that slide.

Doris sighed. "Not well, really. I liked her bookstore, and would shop there, mainly for gifts for the kids. It was a lovely little store."

The kids were Doris' grandchildren, of which there were three.

"You know," Doris continued. "You have no idea how hard it is to be a single woman of her age around here. I mean, I have Cynthia and her kids. But Carol didn't have that. She was a brave soul." She stopped and looked at Dan.

Dan nodded, but didn't really know what else to say.

"People think you must be lonely, and you are, but not for romance," Doris continued. "You'd just like a few friends, a support group. But nobody wants to hang out with old ladies." Again she looked at Dan.

Dan smiled. "Doris, I'm happy to hang out with you any time," he said gently.

"I'm not joking," she answered angrily.

Dan held up his hands. "I'm not joking either, Doris. Really."

"Oh, I know," Doris said. "And like I said, I have Cynthia and her kids. They bless me every day. But Carol didn't have that. She had a bookstore. A store she ran all by herself—took on all that responsibility. She had employees to manage. And money to manage. And nobody thinks old ladies can do that. But she did it."

Dan nodded. "Was it profitable?"

"I suppose," Doris agreed. "It was a going concern. She made it that way. She had a hell of a time with the bank when she started. She told me that. But once it opened, there were always a few customers inside. And she worked with State Park, too, to carry stuff that would work for the tourists. She really worked very hard to make that store work."

"And then she just disappeared?" Dan asked.

"That's what they say," Doris said grimly. "I'm not sure they really looked that hard. No next of kin, and an old lady. You heard what Cal said. Her employees were out of a job, but I don't think they raised much of a stink. And they claimed that there was money missing from the till—if they didn't take it themselves."

"I have to think that Cal would be pretty conscientious in checking that stuff out," Dan said.

"Oh, of course," Doris agreed. "But she lived here, and her car was in Calaveras County, so at first there was a big fuss about who was investigating. And in the end, nobody found anything. And nobody found Carol."

A car pulled up in the parking lot, and Dan and Doris both turned to look.

"Well, anyway," Doris said. "She deserved something better."

"Do you want to help these people?" Dan asked gently, pointing to the group outside. "I can do it."

"No, I'll be fine," Doris said, taking off her glasses and dabbing briefly at her eyes and nose with a tissue. "I'll talk to these people. You better call Cal and tell him that Carol Lawlor's car is up here."

chapter 18

Cal Healey was not amused when Dan told him about the car. "You're shitting me," were his exact words.

Dan assured him he was not.

Cal asked Dan to go out and check on the car and call him back.

Dan walked out into the bright sunlight of the parking lot and strolled over to the car. The car was clean and shiny, even down to the tires. He could even see where a bumper sticker had been removed from the back panel of the trunk, leaving a neat square of slightly brighter paint. Dan peered through the windows and saw that the doors were unlocked.

He pulled out his bandanna and opened the door. Inside, the car had been cleaned, and it still looked nicely detailed. Dan peered under the dashboard and pulled the hood release. Then he walked around to the front of the car and struggled for a few minutes, trying to find the latch in the grill. As he did this, he noticed a few handprints on the front of the hood. Once he found the latch, he lifted the hood, and checked.

There was no battery in the car.

But to Dan's eyes, the cables there looked cleaner, as if they had been moved, while the rest of the engine compartment looked like a ten-year old car. He dropped the hood with a bang and went back in to call Cal.

Cal didn't try to hide his frustration. "We have better things to do than to chase this fucking car down every few days," he said.

Dan was puzzled. "If they were trying to steal it, they wouldn't leave it in such obvious places," he said to Cal.

"Or they ran out of gas, or they were just out joyriding" Cal added. "And you know what? I don't really give a damn."

"But somebody must have a key to this thing, right?" Dan asked him. "What about the bookstore employees?"

"Apparently not," Cal replied. "No, let me rephrase that. Apparently, somebody does."

Dan told him about the battery cables.

"Yeah, we checked that," Cal said. "The first time we picked it up, we checked the mileage. It was about what you would expect if you drove it up from her house to Pinecrest. Which indicates they didn't just tow it. Somebody is driving this thing."

Dan asked about the neighbors, who might have seen something.

"Well, it's not actually at her house," Cal said. "They've been parking it in the parking area by the market. I'm beginning to think I need to tell them to have somebody watch the damn thing 24/7."

"You know, for a car that's been left in a parking lot for a while, it looks really clean," Dan said.

"Yeah," Cal agreed. "I noticed that last time. So somebody steals a car with no battery, and washes it and fills it up before they leave it somewhere."

"Nice car thieves." Dan laughed. "I should leave mine unlocked more often. Maybe they'd clean it and fill up that tank."

"And they do a good job cleaning it," Cal agreed.

"I was going to suggest that it was to remove fingerprints," Dan said. "But there are a couple of big handprints right on the hood."

"Well, that's something," Cal said begrudgingly.

Dan suggested that they could put an alarm on the car. "That might discourage the thieves. Or you could put one of those Denver boots on it."

"I'm gonna tell this attorney that the car is in danger of becoming a liability issue," Cal said. "Get him to put a 'club' on it or something. Attractive nuisance, right?"

That was the second time Dan had heard that phrase recently, or maybe the third. He was about to make a smart aleck remark when Doris caught his eye and motioned that he had another call. He wished Cal luck and turned to Doris.

"It's Chris Martin from the Eldorado," Doris explained. "I hope you don't mind…"

Dan switched to the other line and greeted Chris. "How's life with you?" he asked.

"Just thought you might like an update on the Mokelumne Canyon stuff," Chris said.

Dan grinned. "I'd love it." He quickly brought Chris up to date on his research, including his conversation with Hoss Adams.

"I don't know how much those guys can tell you," Chris said. "Or it would be better to say that I don't know how much you can trust what they do tell you. They are not always completely accurate, at least in my experience."

Dan explained that at this point they hadn't really told him anything, except to never wear red to his first meeting.

"Yeah, I've heard that too," Chris said. "It's all a bit too juvenile for my taste."

Dan asked him if he had anyone else work on the trail down into the canyon since their own expedition.

"Yeah, there was a group of two or three people who went down there yesterday," he said. "I only got a sketchy report, but it doesn't sound like they got a lot done."

"You should pay them less," Dan said.

"The volunteers? Yeah, good idea," Chris agreed. "Or at least cut their benefits."

Dan chuckled. "Cut those benefits back to the roots," he said. "Just like lopping on the trail."

"Well, that's what they were supposed to be doing," Chris said. "Remember that upper section, before you get to Deer Creek? They were going to go in there and clean that out."

"And they didn't get it done?" Dan asked.

"I guess not," Chris said. "I don't know. Somebody was late, so they didn't start on time. And then somebody forgot to bring tools, so they only had two loppers for three people."

Dan laughed. "Sounds like us on a good day."

"Exactly," Chris agreed. "Only we still manage to get something done. A lot done. These people didn't."

"Still, with three people working, and two pairs of loppers, they should have been able to finish off that section," Dan insisted. "It was only a couple of hours of work, right?"

"Yeah…" Chris sounded doubtful. "Maybe more than that. But I guess they just got discouraged or something. I don't know. They just told me that they were sorry, but they didn't get it done. And they weren't really excited about going back to finish it another time."

"Well, I don't know when you want to get back in there again," Dan said. "But I'd be up for it. And I'm sure we could clear out that brush pretty quickly."

"Yeah," Chris said. "But if you and I go back there, I want to work further down into the canyon. That brush isn't really bad, and we can get that some other time. But the section down below is a lot worse. A lot worse. And a lot more interesting."

Dan laughed. "Sounds perfect. When do we start?"

"I was wondering what your schedule was like next week…" Chris offered. "I mean, if you still want to do it. I'm furloughed, so I can go with whatever works for you."

"Let me think about it, and get back to you," Dan said. "I mean, I'd love to do it. I like working with you, and we get a lot done. And that area is now on my radar. I want to spend more time there. But I have to check out what else is going on. Right now, I'd have to say Wednesday and Thursday…"

Chris was clearly delighted. "Great. As long I get furloughed this next week, you can pick your dates and we'll go."

chapter 19

Since Dan had finished writing up his reports, his next week was relatively open, at least on the work side of things. He had saved up a few days of comp time over the previous few months, and Steve Matson didn't have any problem with him using them during the week, when things were quiet at the ranger station. That would all change the following week, when the schools got out and the tourists started arriving in big numbers.

But Dan didn't tell him where he was going, he just said he was taking a couple of days of R&R before the big crush of the season, and Steve agreed. Dan wondered if Steve guessed where he was going, but since Steve didn't ask, and Dan didn't tell, it looked like they were both willing to leave things well enough alone.

He wondered if he was being a little too obsessive about the canyon. He had called that guy back, the one who had called the ranger station, and given him more information. But the guy had already decided to hike somewhere else and didn't seem very interested in what Dan had to say. He did thank Dan, though, for following up. At least that was something.

When Dan got home that night, he dialed Kristen's number, but since she didn't answer, Dan had to leave a message. He told her about the trip and then, on impulse, he invited her along.

Why had he done that? Maybe to compensate. Would she be

angry that he wasn't keeping those days open to spend with her? As he thought about it, he worried that maybe he had sounded too abrupt, as if he had decided that he was going, and she could come along or not, which didn't sound quite right. He thought about calling her back and clarifying things, but finally decided that he could explain just as well when she returned his call.

He heated up some pizza from the night before, added a big salad, and sat down to watch the news and wait for Kristen to call.

The news depressed him. Even the local news was full of car accidents and murders, and he turned it off after about twenty minutes, first checking through the channels to make sure that there was nothing else he wanted to watch. There wasn't.

He walked out into the backyard of his house, trying to remember if Kristen had told him that she had a job that night. He knew she had told him about a few things in her schedule, but he couldn't remember exactly which days.

He thought about giving her another call, if only to clarify his message, but decided that it was too late for that. It would sound as if he had worried about it all evening. Which, he realized, was close to the truth. But it wouldn't do to have her know that. He was desperate to keep her from thinking he might be that desperate.

When he was younger Dan would have been eager to find any excuse to spend more time with Kristen, to charm her, to somehow convince her that he was a great guy, in the hopes that she would agree. He remembered that feeling, the exhausting but exhilarating chase. But he was older now. He knew that the chase was not the point. And somewhere in his gut he knew that Kristen would resist that. Pushing harder would only push her away.

But that didn't make this any easier.

He couldn't stop thinking about her. That was obvious. And

she seemed to feel the same way. They had made love. He certainly wasn't seeing anyone else, and he didn't think she was, either.

But there was always a sense of distance from Kristen. She would withdraw just when Dan thought things were going really well, as if every time they were paddling the canoe in rhythm, and really getting somewhere, she stopped and got out for a few minutes. And left him sitting in the canoe.

It was frustrating. But Dan knew the one thing he couldn't do was express that frustration to Kristen. He didn't want to convince her, to sell her on the idea. He knew that she would have to find her own way back into the canoe. And each time he had to wait for that to happen. Which was what he was doing right now—what he thought he was doing.

Dammit.

The sun had set but it was still light outside, and Dan heard, off in the distance, someone firing a gun, probably over in the National Forest a few blocks away. "Exercising their second amendment rights," was what his elderly neighbor called it, with a smirk.

The noise of the gunfire, combined with the bright light that his uphill neighbor turned on at dusk, chased Dan back inside the house, but not before he was delighted to note the first bat of the evening, swirling magically around through the pines. He stopped to admire it for a few minutes before going inside.

Dan turned on his computer to see an email from Chris. It was an open invitation, copying about ten people, and inviting them to join Chris on a trail crew project down into the Mokelumne Canyon next Wednesday and Thursday.

Dan felt a twinge of irritation as he read the email. He hadn't confirmed those days with Chris, and now they were written in stone in the email. He decided to write it off as pure enthusiasm from

Chris, but he made a mental note to be a little more careful making plans with Chris.

The phone rang and Dan was slightly disappointed to see that it was Cal Healey calling him.

"Got time for a quick call?" Cal asked him. When Dan agreed, Cal went on to ask him a few questions about Carol Lawlor's car when it had been left outside the ranger station. "So you didn't see anyone around the car?" Cal asked. "What time was this again?"

Dan explained that Doris had gone on her break, and Hoss Adams had come into the station at the same time, around 2:30. He hadn't noticed the car beforehand, but couldn't swear it hadn't been there. He knew it wasn't there in the morning at eight when he had arrived…but that was about all.

Cal asked if Doris had noticed anything. Dan gave him Doris' number, but also told him that she only noticed the car when she returned from her break.

Cal met this news with silence.

"You still there?" Dan asked.

"Hm? Yeah," Cal replied. Another silence. "I'm just trying to figure out what the hell's is going on with this car—if there is somebody up there who is taking it…"

Dan thought this over. "If they were going to the lake, they'd park it there, wouldn't they?" he asked. "I mean, once at Dodge Ridge, and once at our office. It doesn't make sense."

"You got that right," Cal agreed.

"Did you get anything from those prints?" Dan asked.

"Good prints, but nothing in the system," Cal replied.

"And she didn't have any next of kin?" Dan asked again.

Cal paused. "I wonder," he said. "Maybe I'll check that again."

Dan's phone beeped to let him know he had another call, and he begged off quickly. It was Kristen.

"Hello?"

"Hi, Dan, I got your message," Kristen said.

"Yeah," Dan said, "I wanted to explain."

"No, that's okay," Kristen interrupted him. "I just called to say that it's fine."

She sounded cautious, maybe a bit down.

"I could bail on it," Dan assured her. "If there's something you wanted to do…"

"No, that's fine," Kristen said. "It will be good to have a couple of days of down time…"

Dan felt a pang somewhere inside. He hoped Kristen didn't think of him taking up her time, that time away from him was "down time."

"Are you sure?" he asked. He wasn't quite sure what else to say.

"I'm sure," Kristen said. "I'll see you when you get back."

Dan couldn't help feeling that their good-byes were a bit less warm than usual. He hoped it was only his imagination. And he made a promise to handle things differently next time.

Dammit.

chapter 20

When Dan arrived at the trailhead on Wednesday morning, Chris was there, waiting for him in a beat-up Ford van. Dan waved to him and pulled in to park next to the van. There were no other cars around.

Dan grabbed his pack and set it at the base of a large Ponderosa pine near his truck.

Chris was eating a banana, and he climbed out to greet Dan. "It looks like it is just going to be the two of us," he said.

"Did you scare everyone else away?" he asked Chris.

"I guess I did," was the reply. "There may be a couple of people who hike down to join us, but I doubt it."

Chris opened the back doors of the van, exposing a collection of tools and gear enough for six or eight people.

"What are we going to need?" Dan asked.

"Whatever we leave in the van, that's what we'll need," Chris answered. "It never fails." He pulled a shovel and a McLeod out of the van, and handed the shovel to Dan. "Can you take this?" he asked.

Dan nodded. They each pulled a pair of loppers out of the van, and Chris picked up the big two-man buck saw.

"Do you think we'll need this?" he asked.

"Not for the first few miles," Dan said. "But after that?"

Chris sighed and hefted the saw. Dan picked up a smaller hand saw and showed it to Chris. "We should be able to get through a lot of stuff with this," he said.

Chris was staring at the buck saw. "There are some big trees down there," he said.

They pulled out the tools and started packing up. Dan took the smaller saw and loppers and tied them onto his pack. He would carry the shovel in his hand. Chris took a while longer to rope the big bucksaw onto his pack, fussing and pulling and tightening. Then he gave Dan a quick glance.

"Ready to go?" he asked.

Dan pulled on his pack, grunting a bit from the extra weight, grabbed the shovel, and followed Chris down the trail.

The two men made excellent time as they hiked down to Deer Creek. There was still some lopping work to be done in this section, they noted, but the work that had been done over the past trips made this hike easy.

But when they got to Deer Creek, Chris stopped.

Ahead of them, they could see the trail that the team had outlined with stones less than two weeks ago. But now the rock work had all been destroyed. Instead of outlining the trail, the rocks were scattered randomly, most of them in the trail path rather than along the sides.

Chris shook his head disgustedly. "Who the hell would bother to do something like that?" he asked rhetorically.

Dan snorted. "It actually took them some time to do that," he said. "Somebody actually had to work hard to mess it up that much."

Chris agreed, shaking his head. "You gotta wonder about some people…"

But once they got to the creek itself, the log bridge was still in place, and so were a few cairns marking the path.

Dan pointed to the water. "It's lower than it was just last week," he said. "The snowpack is melting down."

The log bridge was now at least six feet above the water.

"You almost don't need the bridge," Chris agreed, as he balanced his way across the log.

Dan followed him, and the two had hiked down another mile or so when Chris called a halt.

"I thought we could camp here," he said. "There's a lot of work to do below here, but this is a better spot to camp."

They set up camp, the tents some fifty feet apart, and both well away from the river. But they could see a deep pool lay just below them, and then a series of small rapids and riffles led the river down into the granite of the gorge.

Dan was the first to finish and walked over to Chris' tent. Without any conversation, the two rangers had left a flat area between the two tents to serve as the camp kitchen and dining room. A large log would serve as both a windbreak for their stoves and seating for their meals.

Chris was quick to finish setting up. "I think we'll leave the big saw here for now," he said. "If we hit some big trees, we can deal with those tomorrow. Let's just see how much we can get done without it today."

Dan nodded. "Should I bring a lunch?" he asked. "Or are you thinking we'll come back here before then?"

"Yeah," Chris said. "Let's take a lunch. I'll add a couple of bottles of water."

Dan offered to bring along his filter, so they could refill down below.

"Sounds good," Chris said. "Let's go see what we can get

done."

As they hiked down the canyon, the trail quickly left the river, and began tracking through the granite ledges and bushes above it on the right-hand side.

The easy part was over.

chapter 21

In less than half a mile, they hit their first snag.

The trail had run along the base of a granite outcropping, between the granite and the river. But here it seemed to come to a halt. A sheet of steep granite led up to the next section of trail—not so steep that you couldn't scramble up it, but at the bottom there was no easy way to get up over a lip of the rock to get on the slope. The lip stood well over head height above them.

They looked around for a cairn, or other sign of where the trail had gone, and didn't find it.

Chris clambered up a series of large cracks, and Dan followed on a slightly different route. Once up on the granite, they could see that the trail continued up and over a large granite ridge.

Chris stopped and surveyed their route and then turned to Dan.

"This is right," he said. "It goes up right through here. But I don't like that part down there." He pointed to the cracks they had climbed.

Dan waved at a couple of boulders below. "We might be able to use some of those,' he said.

Instead of answering, Chris walked back down the granite slope. He stopped at the cracks and peered over the edge.

"Yeah," he said, "we need to do something about this," and dropped down into the cracks.

Dan followed him down, carefully downclimbing.

For the next hour and a half, they stared at the granite, searched for rocks that would fit, tried some that didn't work, fit others into place, and sweated in the sun. They dug out some of the dirt, where there was dirt, to make a better bed for the rocks they were moving into place. They wedged smaller rocks between the rocks to keep things from moving.

Each time they hoisted a large rock in place, they stood back and checked it. Was it flat? Was it stable? Dan climbed up and jumped on it. Chris tried to go up the route with no hands.

Each time they agreed it wasn't good enough. And they turned to see what other rocks were around, which ones they could move, and which ones would fit into place.

The last time Chris went up the route with no hands, he got to the top and said, "I think that works."

Dan, on his knees at the base, was shoving a final wedge into place. "Good enough for me," he said. "But if we're done here, I need some water." He climbed up to join Chris on the ridge. Dan realized that from where they stood, they were only about a hundred yards from the top of the knob, where Chris had once shown him the view over the entire gorge.

"How about we drink up there?" he asked.

Chris smiled. "You remember that, huh?"

The route was easy, and they even found a small tree that offered a bit of shade.

Dan's eyes scanned the massive granite bowl below him. "Where does this trail go from here?" he asked Chris.

Chris pointed back over his right shoulder with his chin. "Back down behind that little ridge. It gets away from the river for a while here. I think there's enough work for us down through that section.

It's really overgrown."

The vista over the canyon was impressive. And quiet.

After a short break, they hopped off the ridge and found the traces of the trail through the granite. A few cairns marked the way, but they also spent some time taking down many other cairns that decades of hikers had put up over the years that led to other routes, maybe a fishing hole, or a campsite. "Cairn chaos," Chris had called it.

Chris looked at Dan. "Do you know what the collective noun for a bunch of cairns is?" he asked.

Dan shook his head.

"A confusion of cairns," Chris said with a chuckle.

Dan laughed. It was time to get back to work.

The two men hiked down to the first brushy section. For a hundred and fifty yards, the trail disappeared into a six-foot wall of dense huckleberry oak.

Chris dropped his pack and tools and said, "Time for lunch."

He turned and looked towards the river. "Let's go over there and eat by the water."

Dan followed him to the river and pulled out his crackers, cheese and salami. Chris, Dan noted, was eating gorp and fresh grapes.

"No wonder your pack weighs so much," he said to Chris. "All that fresh fruit?"

Chris grinned. "Want some?"

Dan didn't think he should accept the offer, after making fun of Chris for carrying it in, so he asked Chris about his family.

"Two daughters and a wife," was the answer. "Not necessarily in that order." They chatted about the girls, and how Chris had met his wife.

"College, or really, the summer after college," Chris said. "We were both working in the garden at the college over the summer...."

The noise of the rushing river washed over them, adding a soothing texture to the conversation.

It took them some time and willpower to pack up their lunch and get back to working on the trail. Finally, Chris pulled out his loppers and said, "Okay, time for more fun."

Dan followed him into the thicket. It was hot, dusty work. The trail was invisible from above, and it was only by looking down, peering below the brush, that they could follow the old tread of the trail.

They whacked and lopped, tossing the cut branches into the canyon below. Once Chris asked to borrow Dan's smaller saw to cut a large branch. Dan was happy to take a break to give him the saw.

After a water break, they manage to cut through the brush, and find the next section of the trail, now back near the river, and crossing over a series of small creeks. By the time they got to the river, Dan suggested that it was time for another water break.

Chris walked out onto the boulders and filtered some water for them both. While he did that, Dan explored along the side of one of the creeks.

A white bone stood out among the dark granite boulders of the creek. Dan picked it up and looked at it.

"Whatcha got there?" Chris asked.

Dan thought it over. "I don't know. I think it's a femur," he said.

Chris came over and looked at the bone. "Looks like a femur to me," he said. "But I don't know from what."

Dan held the bone up to his own leg. "Something smaller than me," he said.

Chris took it from him. "That's not saying much," Chris

chuckled. "But it's smaller than me. I don't know. A deer? A calf? It could be a calf."

Dan shook his head. "I don't know. I think a cow or a calf would be thicker," he said. He looked around at the steep granite. "It would take some effort for a cow to get down here."

"It would take even more for a cow to get out," Chris responded.

Dan left the bone on the ground and joined Chris down by the river.

chapter 22

"Do they run cattle down here?" Dan asked.

Chris nodded. "It's a money-losing proposition. The only reason they do it is because they would forfeit their ancestral rights if they didn't keep doing it. But they lose money on it every year."

Dan nodded. "Grandfathered in. I met a guy once who offered to raise the money to make a bid on the grazing rights over in the Stanislaus," he said. "He was unhappy to learn that he couldn't bid on them, because he wasn't grandfathered in. So they keep running the cattle, and losing money, and fucking up the wilderness… all for the sake of history."

Chris grinned. "How do you really feel about it?"

"It's true," Dan insisted. "They always lose money on it. The only reason they do it is so that they don't lose the right to keep doing it."

Chris's face gave a grimace. "I can understand that if your family had done this for generations, you would want to keep that alive."

"As a hobby?" Dan interrupted him. "And meanwhile we got cows all over the place, cow shit all over the place, meadows getting trampled into mudholes. All for some guy's hobby."

By now the conversation had led them back to their tools.

"Do you see my loppers anywhere?" Chris asked.

Dan took a quick glance around. "Not here. Did you leave them over by the river?"

"No, I left them here somewhere." Chris began to wander back up the trail a bit.

Dan set to work with his loppers, digging deep into the brush to cut the trunks of the brush that had overwhelmed the trail.

Chris returned in a few minutes.

"Did you find them?" Dan asked.

"No," Chris' answer was curt. "Maybe down here." And he plunged down the trail into the brush.

Dan worked for a few more minutes, then found a thick branch that curled along the ground, supporting a massive cluster of brush. He put down his loppers and pulled out the small saw.

He bent down, face well into the brush, and tried to lift the branch up off the ground so that he could cut it cleanly, without dragging his saw into the dirt. That was a sure way to take the edge of the teeth off the saw. He leaned in on his knees, resting one elbow on the ground. It was dirty work.

Chris appeared, looking frustrated, and picked up Dan's loppers. "I'm going to use yours, if you're using the saw," he said.

"Help yourself," Dan said. "In fact, if you want, you can use those all the time, and I'll just step in when you get to something big enough for the saw."

"Yeah, thanks," Chris replied dryly—maybe more dryly than Dan had hoped.

"You still didn't find them?" he asked.

"Oh, they're around here somewhere," Chris insisted, digging violently into the branches of a bushy oak.

"You'll probably find them right at the end of the day," Dan said. "Just in time to carry them out."

But Chris didn't answer. He just stood up and threw a huge mess of brush down the hill and went back to lopping.

From his knees on the ground, Dan looked up at Chris and pointed to the radio on Chris's belt. "You could always just call in a chopper to deliver another pair of loppers," he said. "But if you do that, ask them to bring in a couple of cold beers, too."

Chris snorted. "Down here? This radio won't work down here. We'd have to get halfway up those cliffs over there before we could get any reception." He was still upset about not finding his tools.

Dan continued to try to make light of the situation, but he could tell that Chris was angry. "Damn," he said. "I didn't really care about the loppers, but I was really looking forward to a couple of beers."

"Yeah, right?" Chris said. "You can have some of my grapes tonight at dinner."

Chris put down the loppers to throw more brush down the hill, and Dan picked them up to take his turn, jabbing into the depths of the brush, then yanking the handles closed, trying to cut through the thicker branches at the base of the brush.

It was hotter now, and Dan was sweating fiercely. His face was covered in dust, and there were dried leaves scattered on his clothes.

Chris watched Dan for a few minutes, and then said. "I think it's time we found a shady spot to work." He edged past Dan and started to push through the brush of the overgrown trail, down into the canyon.

Fifty yards farther along, a large Ponderosa pine shaded the trail. Chris turned and looked at Dan. "Are you okay here?" he asked.

Dan nodded. "Absolutely. It sure beats working in the sun."

"Yeah, that's what I thought." Chris looked further down the trail. "I think I am going to try to push through all of this and see what we have in front of ourselves," he said. "Is that okay?"

Dan grinned. "I'm in the shade. I'm fine. Don't get lost."

Without another word, Chris disappeared, carefully picking his way through the mass of whitethorn to follow the traces of the trail in front of him.

Dan worked slowly in the shade. He had started in the middle of the shade, and now, as the sun headed west, Dan worked east, always staying in the shadow of the huge pine. The pace was just about right, he thought, clearing the trail in rhythm with the turning of the Earth and the passage of the sun.

But it was quiet. Astonishingly quiet. Only the gentle rush of the river below him made any noise. Dan stopped and looked around. He had no real idea where Chris was, other than down the canyon. If something happened to him, Dan wouldn't know for hours. And wouldn't really have a clear idea of what to do about it.

He lopped off another branch of oak, just a bit more carefully this time, and tossed it down the hill. He looked around again, impressed with the sense of solitude. Except for Chris, he doubted that there was anyone else in the canyon. And he was at least five miles in from the trailhead, and the next nearest human.

After an hour or so, Dan decided that he needed a break. It was still hot, even in the shade, and he was feeling dehydrated, drained of energy. Besides, he was working hard enough that he was beginning to get ahead of the shade. And that wouldn't do.

He put down his loppers, pulled off his gloves, and pulled a bottle of water out of his day pack. There wasn't a perfect rock or log to sit on, so he just sat down on the edge of the trail, making sure he was in the heart of the shade of the big pine.

Again, the silence impressed him. There were no animals here, at least not in the heat of the middle of the day. And even the birds seemed to have gone quiet. He wondered what had happened to Chris.

A noise below him caught his attention, something in the brush, and then Chris pushed through into the open part of the trail that Dan had just cleared. Dan considered picking up the loppers and looking busy, but decided it wasn't worth the effort.

Chris looked up at him, pleasantly surprised. "You got a lot done!"

Dan grinned. "I moved at the speed of light. Or maybe just the sun. Or the shade," he said.

Chris surveyed the work. "Looks great."

Dan noticed that Chris still didn't have his loppers and was about to ask about them when Chris spoke.

"There are some huge trees down here across the trail," he said, pointing to the trail behind him. "Really big."

"We've got the saw back at camp," Dan reminded him.

"Yeah," Chris agreed. "But these are three or four feet across. It would take us a long time to get through them. I think we'll leave them for when I can come back here with a bigger crew."

Dan nodded. He knew all too well how much fun it was to cut through a tree like that with only two men. "How many of them are there?" he asked. "We might be able get through them tomorrow."

Chris shook his head. "There are at least two trees, and one of them has fallen right along the path of the trail. It's going to be a ton of work to get those cut through and then get them moved. I think it's more than a two-person job. It would take us most of the day."

"Okay," Dan agreed, picking up his loppers.

"Are you ready for a surprise?" Chris asked him. Something in the way Chris asked the question caught Dan off guard.

Dan stopped. "Sure," he said cautiously.

"So those trees are across the trail," Chris said. "But somebody has cut off all the branches on top, like they were clearing a trail. It's hard to get up on top of them, but once you do, you can just walk along the top of the logs, instead of the trail."

"Huh!" Dan grunted. "How long ago was that?" he asked.

"That's the weird part," Chris said. "These trees must have fallen in the last couple of years."

Dan considered this. "Nice of them to work on the logs, but it would have been even nicer if they had tackled this damn brush."

Chris fixed Dan with a stare. "They did." He paused to let this sink in. "On the other side of these huge trees, this trail has been cleared for a good long way. And in the last couple of years. That's where I was walking."

Dan burst out laughing. "I thought you'd just decided to take a nice long break." Then the import of what Chris had just said sank in. "Who the hell would do that?" he asked. "And why would they wait until they got down to this part to do any work? Why not do the part we just whacked?"

"Yeah," Chris said. "That's exactly what I'm wondering."

Dan looked down the canyon. "Is there another trail they could have taken from the other side?" he asked.

Chris shook his head slowly. "The only one is down Jackass Canyon, and I tried that late last year. It was a complete shit show. Impenetrable." He pointed to the brush behind Dan. "Just like this for miles. I mean, I made it down, but it was a mess."

Dan turned back to face the brush covering the trail. The sun had now reached where he was working, and he would have to shift a few feet to stay in the shade.

Chris noticed and said, "Let's call it a day. We can get back to camp and clean up and come back here tomorrow when it's cooler."

Chris began to look around for his loppers again.

"Do you think an animal could have taken them…for the salt?" Dan asked.

"They're big," Chris exclaimed. "You think a bear did that?"

Dan shook his head. "But maybe a very salt-deprived marmot?"

Chris kept searching, under the brush and back up the trail. But he was losing faith. "Let's just come back tomorrow and I'll find them."

Dan agreed. "We can keep an eye out for them on the way back," he said. "Maybe they're back up the trail somewhere."

"God, I sure hope so," Chris said.

Chris led the way back to camp, stopping from time to time to look at the work they had done and check for his loppers. At one point he took a few minutes to saw through a root that ran across the trail. As they hit a section of granite Dan noticed that Chris missed one of the cairns and drifted off the trail.

That meant that the two of them spent another twenty minutes using a shovel to mark the trail more clearly and moving some downed branches to block off the route that Chris had mistakenly followed.

At the section of granite where they had built up the trail to improve the route over the cracks, Chris stopped again and inspected it.

Dan walked up beside him. "What do you think?"

"It's good," Chris said. "It's not perfect, but it's a lot better than it was."

Dan agreed. They walked down the blocks of rock, testing each one with each step, trying to get them to move.

When Dan got to the bottom, he nodded at Chris. "It's solid."

Chris pointed at the last block. "That one has a little wiggle in it." He bent down and pushed a smaller rock further into the dirt as a wedge.

Dan watched as Chris climbed up on the rock and tried to rock it back and forth. The rock moved very little, but Dan suspected that over time it would get worse, as each new hiker climbed over it.

Chris had hopped down and picked up the shovel. "Fuck it," he said. "Let's go back to camp."

It was only another mile to get there, and with a few more stops, for additional trail work, it took them more than an hour to hike it.

Dan headed straight for his tent to drop his daypack, and then grabbed a bottle of water from the shade and started drinking. He'd been feeling dehydrated all day, and he had decided that when he got back to camp he was going to deal with that once and for all. At least for the rest of the day.

Chris had stacked the tools against a tree, and Dan watched as he picked up a folding bucket and headed down to the river. Chris had said that he liked to rinse off every day in the back country, so Dan left him some space to do that.

Dan pulled off his boots and slid into his tent. He had time for a short rest before dinner, and he eased himself over onto his sleeping pad and stretched out. One by one, he could feel his vertebrae popping as he lay back down on the pad, and he let out a groan with each pop. Bending over to cut that brush had taken a toll.

He stuffed a fleece jacket under his head, closed his eyes, and allowed himself to drift off.

Dan woke up to find that the late afternoon sun was hitting directly on his tent, and the heat was overpowering.

He sat up and zipped open the tent. From where he was, he couldn't see Chris or his tent. Dan crept out of the tent and slipped on his camp shoes.

A quick glance did not show him where Chris was. Maybe in his tent. If he was resting, Dan didn't want to wake him up.

Dan took his bucket down to the river to fill it up for the evening.

As he waded out into the river, the cold of the water made him stop well before it reached his knees. The snowmelt was icy, even down here in the canyon.

Dan filled the bucket and turned around to walk back out again. As he did, he noticed Chris' body lying in the shade on a sandy patch of beach downstream.

By the time Dan had picked his way back onto the bank, Chris looked up. "You ready for dinner?"

Dan nodded and held up his bucket. "This should be enough for us both," he said. "I'll get it started on the filter.'

Chris followed Dan back up to their camp, then walked over to his side of the clearing, where his tent and bear can were.

Dan poured some of the water into his filter bag and hung it back in a tree.

That's when he heard Chris yell. "What the fuck?"

Dan turned to look at him. Chris was holding his bear canister and shaking it.

"This thing feels empty," he said and began to work the top loose.

Dan's stomach gave a jolt. He quickly walked over to his bear can. His can had transparent sides, and he could see there wasn't much food in it. He picked it up and peered through the side. There was no food there.

He turned and looked at Chris, who was holding his can upside down. A few small packets of something—salt? mustard?—fell to the ground. The two men stared at each other.

"Sonofabitch! Some asshole's took our food!" Chris yelled.

Dan took a deep breath. They were four or five miles from the trailhead. They could still make that before dark, easily. And the route would take them past the campsites at Deer Creek. There was just a chance that whoever took their food was camped there.

He mentioned this to Chris.

"I don't think we have a choice," Chris said. "I'm all for roughing it, but I'm not interested in spending the night down here if we don't have anything to eat."

"Or breakfast for tomorrow," Dan added.

"No shit," Chris agreed.

It took them another ten seconds to fully grasp what had happened. Then Dan turned and started taking his camp down. "Don't forget your water system," Chris called to him, pointing to the tree where it hung.

But Dan was looking at his bear can. There didn't seem to be any footprints near it, although the ground might have been brushed to hide them.

"Do you see any footprints around your camp that aren't yours?" he asked Chris.

Chris took a quick look around, then started shaking his head. "I can't tell. It looks like somebody might have covered them up…"

Dan wondered if he should try to protect any fingerprints on his bear can, and then decided that given the current state of law enforcement, this case wasn't going to get any attention anyway. Still he tried to be careful with it.

Within a few minutes the two men had packed up their gear and were ready to hike out. Chris picked up the shovel, and Dan grabbed the McLeod. "This might come in handy at Deer Creek, if we find the guys with our food," he said with a wicked grin.

"Right?" Chris was still outraged. "Fuckin' unbelievable."

They hiked back up the canyon quickly, pushing themselves to hurry as only a couple of rangers can.

But when they got to Deer Creek, there was nobody there.

They took a few minutes to check all the possible campsites, and then gave up. Overhead, they heard the distant cry of an osprey, and stood and watched as it slowly sailed down the canyon, high above the trees, searching for fish in the river.

"It's looking for dinner, too," Chris suggested.

Dan nodded. "I'll bet it has better luck than we do."

It was another two miles to the trailhead, and they hiked them in silence.

chapter 24

"Hi." Kristen's subdued greeting on the phone surprised Dan, and it took him a moment to recover.

"Hi." he finally replied. "How are you doing?"

"Okay," she reassured him, still quiet. "Fine, I guess."

"Are you sure?" he asked, offering a tiny chuckle to encourage her.

"Yeah." A long pause. "Just dealing with some stuff here."

Dan considered this. "Anything I can help with?" he asked.

"No," Kristen was quick to respond. She waited a bit, then continued. "Just stuff that happened a long time ago."

"Okay," Dan said this guardedly. He wanted to offer more, to know more, but wasn't quite sure how to do that.

"I'm okay," she said, this time with more vigor. "How was your trip?"

Dan had wanted to tell her all about it, but now worried that she might find the details trivial. He gave her a quick summary, ending with the missing food and their reason for coming back early.

"That's horrible," Kristen responded. "What kind of person would take your food?"

As they talked through the details of the trip, Kristen became more animated. Soon she was urging Dan to report the theft to the sheriff's office.

"I don't think Cal would appreciate that." Dan said. "Besides, this was in Calaveras County, so it's outside his jurisdiction. And twenty bucks' worth of food isn't exactly Grand Theft."

Kristen was adamant. "It's not a lot of money, but it could have been really serious," she said. "And what if it happened to someone else?"

Dan downplayed this. "We were hungry, and we were only four miles in. There is a big difference between being hungry and starving. We weren't starving. We just had to cut our trip short by a day. Plus, whoever did it must have hiked out right away. Not much chance of it happening again."

But in the end, Kristen got Dan to promise her that he would at least mention the incident to Cal. "It may not be serious, but someone who would take your food might also do worse things…"

Dan grudgingly admitted that she might be right.

They ended the call with a promise to talk again in a couple of days.

But before Dan called Cal, he thought it might be best to call Chris Martin. It had been Chris' trip, after all, and Dan didn't feel right stepping on his toes.

He decided that call could wait until after he'd read his emails. There might even be one from Chris.

Half an hour later his phone rang.

"Hey there," Cal Healey greeted him. "I hear you've been having some adventures. Seems like you are always the victim."

Dan laughed. "Hi, Cal. Yeah, Grand Theft Bear Can in the Mokelumne Wilderness." He chuckled again. "Did Kristen call you?"

"Nope," Cal said. "Maggie called Kristen to invite her to dinner, and Kristen told Maggie."

"Geez. This is such a small town," Dan said. "News travels fast."

"Especially when it's bad," Cal agreed. "Can you come to dinner two weeks from Thursday?"

Dan made a show of checking his calendar, but he knew he was free. "Yep—got it noted. Anything I can bring?"

"No," Cal assured him. "You know Maggie. She's got it all covered."

Dan knew that this meant he would bring Maggie some flowers, as he usually did. She seemed to appreciate those, at any rate.

"So?" Cal asked. "What the hell happened?"

Dan laughed again, and told Cal the bare bones of his trip with Chris into the canyon.

When he finished, Cal said, "The mysteries of Mok Canyon will never end."

"That's because law enforcement up here has better things to do," Dan suggested. "At least, that's true of the Forest Service."

"Not always," Cal answered. "Sometimes we have to take a trip into the wilderness, just to make sure that our local rangers aren't falling asleep on the job."

"Cal, if you want to come with me the next time I do trail work, I would love to have you," Dan said with all sincerity, but also knowing there wasn't a chance in hell that Cal would do that.

"Thanks, but no thanks," Cal said. "My knees are painful enough already. I'm not that good with a shovel, anyway,"

"I was thinking you could tackle the whitethorn, down on your knees, lopping brush," Dan said. "It would build character."

"Fuck you," Cal laughed. Then dropped his voice. "Oops. Maggie heard that. The kids are home."

"I think we're going back there next week," Dan said. "We

want to try and finish off that section of the trail."

"You might consider taking a break," Cal suggested. "You're getting just a bit obsessive compulsive about that canyon."

Dan laughed. "I like Chris, and I like working with him. We're a good team out there."

"Uh huh." Cal was unimpressed. "Don't you get enough of that stuff in your day job?"

"That's the thing," Dan explained. "I've spent so much time this summer behind the desk, it feels good to get out and do something in the forest. And with my hands."

"Hell, I have a whole backyard you could work on," Cal suggested. "Pruning, mowing. Maggie wants to put in a small fountain and a pond. You could do the digging."

"Not the same." Dan replied. "Besides, tracking down the old route of this trail is fun. It's a bit like solving a mystery. You find cuts in the brush that somebody made twenty or thirty or forty years ago. And the stonework that's still there, sometimes, underneath everything else. It's cool."

"All of that in my backyard," Cal said. "And I'll even supply the tools."

Cal's mention of tools reminded Dan, and he told Cal about Chris and the missing loppers.

"So, two full-grown rangers go on a hike, lose valuable US government property, and get robbed, all within twenty-four hours?" Cal asked. "It's a miracle we have any trees left."

Dan laughed and asked Cal to thank Maggie for the dinner invitation.

Cal promised he would. But before he hung up the phone, he asked Dan about his bear canister. "It's plastic, right? Did you open it after you noticed the food was gone?"

"No reason to," Dan explained. "It's transparent. I could see the food was gone."

"If you want, bring it down to the station, and we can run it for prints."

Dan laughed. "I don't think it's worth it. Not for what they stole."

"See?" Cal asked. "That's why you're not in law enforcement. Sometimes we don't measure the crime in dollars. Sometimes we just want to know what's going on…"

"This was in Calaveras County," Dan reminded him.

"Yep." Cal agreed. "Right on the border with Tuolumne County. Seriously, Dan. We have a couple of local goons here that we think are screwing up big time, but we don't have the hard evidence we need to collar them. If their prints are on your can, then maybe we can make them sweat a little."

"You think these guys are driving all over the foothills stealing stuff?" Dan asked. "Like that car?"

"Among other things, yes," Cal replied. "And we would like to think we can make sure it stops."

Dan shrugged his shoulders. "Okay. I'll bring the can by tomorrow, sometime late in the day. I have a meeting that I can use as an excuse."

"Sounds typical," Cal said. "Just leave it at the front counter and I'll get it."

"Will do," Dan agreed. "But first I'll give it a good washing tonight. Just to make sure it's clean."

"Good idea," Cal agreed. "And rub it down carefully with a towel afterwards to make sure it's nice and dry."

Dan ended the call with a chuckle, then went to retrieve his bear canister from his pack. This time he would put on gloves.

chapter 25

The bear canister didn't make it immediately to Cal's desk.

For one thing, he was out in the field most of the day, and when Dan dropped off the canister it was put in a bag with Cal's name on it behind the counter at the Sheriff's office. So it was a few days later that someone working the counter noticed it, and sent Cal a note about it.

That happened to be on Cal's day off.

Once back in the office, he worked his way through some paperwork, and left the bear canister for later. He would have to get it over to the lab, and that meant more paperwork. And there was a burglary in Jamestown that got his attention first.

And then that damn car appeared again, this time in the parking lot of the high school.

But Cal thought it was important enough to stay a few minutes late that day to fill out the forms and start it on its way to the lab.

Which isn't to say that it got immediate attention there.

Tuolumne County shares a lab with a few other neighboring counties, and it generally runs a few days to a few weeks behind, depending on who needs what, and when they need it.

In fact, Cal had forgotten all about the bear canister when Dan called him a few days later.

"Any chance you guys are done with that yet?" Dan asked him.

Cal exhaled loudly into the phone. "I have no idea. Let me check on it for you," he told Dan. "When do you need it back?"

"Today," Dan said, with a chuckle. "I've got a trip coming up, and it's time to start packing."

"That ain't gonna happen," Cal said. "It's down in Ripon at the lab. Sorry."

"That's Okay. I've got another one," Dan said. "But it's just a bit bigger and heavier."

"That will do you good," Cal said. "More exercise that way."

"Thanks," Dan said dryly.

"I'll give them a call and see if I can move things along," Cal said. "Sometimes they need a little nudge."

"Sounds like some other people I know." Dan suggested.

"And it's nice talking to you, too," Cal replied.

Later that morning, Cal called down to the lab, and asked them about the bear canister.

As he suspected, they hadn't done anything with it yet, but they promised to get around to it in the next couple of days. Cal thanked them and sent Dan a text to update. "Enjoy the hike. You'll have your can back in time for the next one."

But first thing in the morning, a couple of days later, when the lab director called Cal, he launched straight into the conversation without even the pleasantries of hello and how are you.

"Where did you get this bear can?" the lab director asked Cal.

Cal suggested that he could find that information on the form, then told him about Mokelumne Canyon.

This was followed by a long silence at the other end, which Cal took it upon himself to break.

"What's going on?" he asked. "Did you get some prints off it?"

"Oh, we got prints," the lab director said. "Do you know a guy up there called Dan Courtwright?"

Cal sighed. "Read the paperwork. It was his can. He brought it in because someone stole some food out of it."

"Well, that explains his prints. And I can tell you who might have taken the food," the lab director said. "An excellent right thumb print, and a middle finger as well. Very clear."

"So?" Cal asked. "Sounds like they are in the system…"

"Oh yeah," the lab director agreed. "The FBI is looking for this guy. He's on their list. Donald Lamar Graham. Major bad news."

The hairs on the back of Cal's neck stood up. "Those were the prints on the bear canister?" he asked.

"Yep," the lab director confirmed. "And a couple of partials that also help."

"Shit," Cal said.

"I thought you might want to know about this," the director said.

Cal thanked him and got off the phone immediately.

First, he went in to tell his boss what he had just learned. The door was open, and Cal quickly walked inside and explained where Dan had left the bear canister.

After a short discussion, they agreed to call in the FBI immediately. "This is one of their top targets," his boss said. "Nice work. I'll let them know. They probably want to talk to you, so stick close to the office today."

Cal agreed and went back to his desk. He stared at his computer screen for a few minutes, without paying much attention to anything he was seeing. His mind was racing, and he walked over to the coffee machine and poured himself a cup.

When he got back over to his desk, he thought he might give Dan a call, and let him know what they had found. It might make the ranger's day.

But when he called the Summit Ranger Station, Doris told him that Dan was off for a few days.

"Oh, that's right," Cal remembered. "He was going on a hike, right?"

"I don't know," Doris said. "He didn't tell me what his plans were."

Cal's stomach suddenly lurched. "Was he going to do some trail work or something?" he asked Doris.

"I'm sorry Cal," Doris answered. "He didn't say."

The churning in Cal's stomach got worse.

He thanked Doris and called Dan's cell phone. No answer, just voice mail. He left a short message, then sent Dan a text to call him ASAP.

A few minutes later, he decided to call Kristen. After five rings, just when Cal was about to hang up, she answered. Cal didn't want to worry her unnecessarily, but he was getting worried himself.

"Hi, Kristen," he said. "It's Cal Healey here. Do you happen to know where Dan might be?"

"He's somewhere in the back country," she said. "He'll be back tomorrow night."

"Do you know where he went, exactly?" he asked.

"No…" Kristen thought about this. "Maybe meeting up with someone to do some trail work?"

"Okay, Thanks," Cal said. "If you could try to get a hold of him, ask him to give me a call. It's pretty important. Something to do with a case I'm on."

Kristen agreed to do that, and Cal sat back in his chair and let himself stew for a few minutes.

Maybe more than a few minutes.

"Son of a bitch!" he said. And he got up, walked back into his boss' office, and closed the door behind himself.

chapter 26

Which was just about the time that Dan and Chris were meeting each other at the Hermit Valley trailhead, ready to hike and set up camp.

While they had been making progress on the trail clearing, there really weren't any good campsites below, so they were planning on camping, as usual, at the campsite by the river below the crossing of Deer Creek. They even knew which tent would go where when they arrived.

But Dan was surprised to see a young woman with Chris this time.

"This is my daughter, Alex," Chris explained. "She has a couple of days off from school, and thought she'd like to join us."

Dan shook her hand and asked her where she was going to school.

"The JC," Alex said, dismissively. "Just taking a few classes while I figure out what I really want to do."

Dan looked at Chris. "Sounds like me at her age," he said.

Chris grinned. "It took me a lot longer than two years to figure it out," he agreed.

Dan's phone beeped at him from inside his truck. He went to pick up it and saw that it was a call from Cal Healey. But as he tried to answer he couldn't hear Cal at all. After a minute of frustration, he quit the call and dropped the phone into his shirt pocket.

Once again Chris and Dan discussed what tools they would need. They decided to bring the big saw, and they promised each other that they would at least try to tackle those big logs on the lower part of the trail.

Dan unconsciously felt for his gloves in his pack. He knew what hours on that saw could do to his hands without the gloves.

His phone beeped again, this time to tell him he had a message. Once again, he tried to connect, but could only hear a garbled note from Cal about calling him back.

He looked into his truck. His radio was there, and he picked it up and tried to call dispatch.

"You're not going to get through from here," Chris said. "At least, I never can."

As he got no response from the radio, Dan shrugged and put it back in the truck. He joined Chris in dividing up the tools, then the three of them shouldered their packs and started down the trail. As they walked past the sign at the trailhead, Dan said, "Advance backcountry skills required, Alex. Better be on your toes."

Chris laughed. "Don't worry about her, Dan. She's been hiking these trails since she could walk."

Alex quickly took the lead, and not long after was already well ahead of the two rangers.

"That's the problem with young people," Dan explained. "They don't realize that they are hiking too fast for us old guys."

"Right?" Chris agreed. "It's okay. She'll wait for us at Deer Creek."

"It must be nice to have her join us." Dan suggested.

"I figured that you wouldn't mind," Chris said. "I don't get to see her as much as I would like to, and when she offered to come along, I jumped at it."

"I think it's great," Dan said. "And we can always use the help."

"Oh, she isn't going to do any work," Chris explained quickly. "That was part of the deal. She said she'd come along if she didn't have do any work."

Dan laughed. "Okay, fine. But just remember that I said the same thing…"

It was a perfect day in the Sierra. The sun was warm, but stepping out of the sun into the shade was immediately cooler. There was not a cloud in the intensely blue sky, and there was only the slightest hint of a breeze. Dan hoped that as the day warmed up, that breeze would increase just enough to keep them refreshed as they worked. Maybe it was something more than just a hope.

At Deer Creek, just as Chris had suggested, Alex was waiting by the log bridge.

"So this is the famous bridge, huh?" she said to her dad.

"That's it," he admitted.

"It's pretty good," Alex said begrudgingly.

"We were going to put a railing on it," Dan teased her, "but we thought you'd prefer the challenge of going across without it."

Alex quickly stepped up onto the log and danced across it.

"Ten years of ballet classes," Chris murmured to Dan.

"Twelve!" Alex shouted over her shoulder, and then started off down the trail to the campsite.

The two rangers finally caught up with her again at the campsite.

"Is this where you meant?" she asked Chris.

"This is it," Chris agreed. "Pick your spot for your tent."

Dan had already set his pack down in its usual place, and Chris walked over to drop his on the far side of the clearing.

"I think I'll go over here," Alex said from the far side of a large, downed tree behind Chris' tent. "That way I won't have to listen to you guys snoring."

It was only late morning when they were ready to get to work. With the tents set up they packed a lunch and grabbed the tools for the morning's work.

"I thought we'd go down and try to get through at least one of those big trees today," Chris said. "Maybe leave the other one for tomorrow, or just clear some brush."

It was another mile or so down the canyon to get to the downed trees, and they stopped to clear a little brush on the way. By noon they were ready to eat, and Alex had decided to join them for lunch. She had walked over to the river to filter some water for everyone, and they chose a spot with a collection of granite boulders in the mixed shade of a huge pine to eat.

"This is where you thought you lost your loppers," Dan said to Chris.

Chris looked around. "Somewhere around here."

Dan could see that this comment had caught Alex's attention, and her eyes began to comb the area.

"We gave it a pretty good search last time," he said to her.

She smiled. "Just checking. I know how you are about your car keys. Maybe I can find these, too."

Chris shook his head in disbelief, remembering the incident. "Hey, if you can find them, great!"

As Alex looked around, she asked, "So where does the trail go from here?"

"Down the canyon," her dad answered, pointing with his sandwich. "Over some big trees, and then more down the canyon."

"Cool. I'll check it out after lunch," Alex said.

chapter 27

Lunch for Dan was his usual: crackers with some salami and cheese, and then a little dried fruit. He was amused to see that Alex followed her father's example. She pulled out peanut butter, bread, some grapes, and an orange. And Chris added in two apples.

"Man, you guys bring real food, don't you?" Dan kidded them.

"Gotta eat healthy," Alex said. "You are what you eat. And your body needs good fuel."

Dan offered them an energy bar from his pack. "Want to try one of these?" he asked.

"Ugh. I mean, no thanks," Alex replied. Chris just shook his head, his mouth being occupied with chewing up a peanut butter sandwich.

Dan put the bar back in his pocket. It might come in handy later. Just then his phone beeped in his pocket. He pulled it out and saw he had another message. This one was from Kristen's number. He tried to connect to his voicemail, but the phone told him he had no service.

"You brought that down here?" Chris asked him, pointing to the phone.

Dan smiled sheepishly. "I forgot it was in my pocket," he admitted. "But I must have got at least some signal somewhere down here."

"Probably bounced off some rocks," Chris said. "Good luck ever finding that spot again."

Dan slipped the phone back into his pocket.

After lunch, the three of them hiked down another mile, to where Dan and Cal had stopped working on their last trip.

"Do you want to tackle one of those logs first?" Dan asked. "Or lop our way down to it?"

Chris thought it over. "We're nice and fresh now," he said. "Let's see if we can get through one of the logs now."

They pushed through the brush, Alex following behind. When they got to the first tree, Dan was surprised at how big it was.

"Damn," he said.

Chris smiled. "Yeah, I told you they were going to take some time." He started to put the handles on the big buck saw.

"Well, it looks like you guys have enough to keep you busy," Alex said. "I think I'll see where this goes from here." And with that she clambered up on top of the log and started to walk along it towards the lower gorge.

"Just be careful," Chris called out. "What time do you want to be back here?"

Dan watched Alex check her watch. "Maybe five?" she suggested

Chris looked at Dan. "We might need to call it quits before then," he said. "What about four?"

Alex thought this over. "Okay. Four-thirty at the latest."

"Remember, you're on your own down there," Chris reminded her.

"Okay. Yes Dad." This last one with an inflection only an adult daughter can add.

Chris chuckled, then looked at Dan. "She'll be fine. You ready to get to work?"

Dan gave a sigh. "I can hardly wait."

But they didn't start sawing immediately. First they had to clear away the brush to give themselves a place to stand on either side of the tree. And then they had a short discussion of exactly how they would cut through the first time, at an angle that would release any tension on the rest of the tree, and still allow them to make a second cut to roll the cut section out of the way, opening up the trail. It took some time to come to agreement on that.

But Chris finally made the call on how and where, and set the saw on top of the tree. "Ready?" he called.

Dan grabbed the handle on the other side of the tree and nodded. They were in full sun, and it was going to be hot work.

The first few minutes of sawing were easy. The bark was soft, and they had cleared some of it away. The sapwood wasn't much harder. And they certainly weren't cutting through the full diameter of the tree. Not yet, anyway.

But fifteen minutes later, the top of the saw was disappearing into the cut, and Dan began to sweat.

After half an hour, Dan calculated that they were about a third of the way through the tree, maybe a bit more, and Chris called a halt. They were now well into the harder heartwood.

"Do you want to switch sides?" Chris asked, "just so we use different muscles?"

Dan looked at the log and considered how much energy it would take to climb over it. "I'm okay," he said. "We can switch for the second cut."

Chris nodded and looked up at the sun. "We should get some shade here in a few minutes."

Dan grinned. "I've been watching it get closer. It should get here just about the time we cut through."

"Perfect for the second cut," Chris said, and grabbed the saw on his side of the tree.

Again they pulled back and forth as a nice pile of sawdust began to accumulate on Dan's side of the tree. But now the sawing got harder as they passed the center of the trunk.

"I think we're binding a bit," Chris said. "Hang on."

Dan used the break to drink more water while Chris pounded a couple of wedges into the top of the cut.

"I was hoping it wouldn't do that," Chris said.

Dan looked at the huge tree. "It's hard to tell. This thing is massive."

They tested the saw, and it now slid through more easily.

Dan had to shift his weight, now that the saw was cutting down into the lower part of the trunk. It wasn't exactly the perfect ergonomic set up, but trail work rarely is. Soon, he and Chris were on their knees in the dirt, still pulling the saw back and forth.

They stopped ten minutes later when Chris suggested that they should clear away some of the dirt underneath the tree, to make room for the saw as it cut through. Dan dug out his side, then took a rest as he passed the shovel over to Chris for him to do the same.

They stopped more frequently now, partly to rest, partly to check on their progress, and partly to see if they could tell exactly what the two parts of the tree would do once they were cut through.

With a tree this size, it wasn't likely that it would move much. But Dan checked both ends of the trunk, just in case. The worst that could happen, he decided, was that the trunk might shift just enough to wedge the saw into place.

Chris stopped again and pounded the wedges a few more times. But they were now under huge pressure and Chris didn't get them to move much at all.

While Chris hammered the wedges, Dan looked at the saw cut one more time.

"We are damn close," he told Chris.

It was only another minute of sawing until the blade broke through. The two men carefully slid the saw out of the cut and stood back to admire their work.

Dan's shoulders were sore, and he could feel the muscles in his back tiring.

"If we cut this through right here," Chris said pointing with his whole arm, "I think we can get it to roll right out and downhill."

"Good plan," Dan said. "Because if it doesn't and it jams up, it's going to be a bitch to move it."

"Yeah," Chris agreed. "Let's not let that happen."

Dan checked his watch. It was two-thirty, and Alex would be back in two hours. It would be nice to get this tree done by then.

chapter 28

Somehow the second cut through the tree was harder. Maybe it was because they took a slightly longer angle through it, to allow it room to move as it fell. Maybe it was because they were tired from the first cut, and just weren't moving with the same energy. Maybe it was because they had subconsciously taken the easier cut first, and were now having to deal with the fact that the ground was less even here.

At any rate, it took them longer.

Chris stopped at one point and asked Dan if he was sorry he had volunteered. "This is damn hard work," he said.

"Nope. Beats working in an office any day," Dan said with a laugh.

"Yeah, but today's our day off," Chris reminded him. "We could be doing something fun."

Dan shook his head. "What could be more fun than this?"

"I could think of a few things," Chris said. "Give me a minute."

Just when they thought they were about through the trunk, one side of the log dropped just a quarter of an inch and wedged itself tightly in place.

Chris mopped the sweat off his forehead with his sleeve and let go of the saw.

"Shit, that doesn't look good," he said.

Dan was panting slightly, still hoping that if they cut through completely the log might fall. He looked around for a branch they could use as a lever in case they needed it.

Dan noticed Chris glancing at his watch.

"What time is it?" he asked.

"Four-thirty," Chris answered. He looked around for Alex, but she was nowhere to be seen.

"Let's finish this cut and see if it will drop through," Dan suggested. "We can't have far to go."

Chris agreed and the two kneeled down to work the big saw. Any suggestion that they might try to stay even a little bit clean was now completely lost. They were kneeling in dirt and breathing in dust and covered in sawdust.

Dan stared at the log, the saw disappearing and the reappearing on his side with each stroke. He was past the point of trying to put a little extra effort into each stoke. He'd passed that point an hour ago. Now he was just hanging on, sharing the load with Chris, and trying not to notice how much his knees hurt. Or his muscles.

He just kept sawing.

The saw slid through the cut, bit into the wood, and the log shifted again. Now it was jammed, held in place by friction from the two sides.

Dan gave a pull, and then realized that Chris was doing the same on his side. "You take it," he said. "I'm going to look for a lever."

He waded into the brush by the side of the tree, looking for a branch that might work. Behind him he could hear Chris grunting as he worked on trying to get the saw loose.

Dan found a branch that he could use, but it would need some work. He went back to join Chris and get the smaller Silky saw to cut off some of the smaller parts of the branch. Chris was now pounding at the wedges, trying to get the log to move just enough to get the saw out. The last thing they wanted to do was to make another cut with the smaller saw, just to free the larger one. That was absolutely the last resort.

In a couple of minutes Dan had the branch cleaned up and got back to Chris just in time to see him slide the saw out from its slot in the tree.

"Cool," Dan said. He held up the branch. "Now all we have to do is get that center section free. This might help."

They wedged the branch under the cut part of the tree and gave a shove, but nothing moved.

"Hang on a second," Chris said. He took the branch and wedged it underneath the other part of the tree. "If we can lift this up," he said, "the part we cut might drop out."

It took them another minute or two to put the plan into place, and then they gave a heave. The cut portion of the trunk slid, stopped, and then, as they gave another heave, dropped free to roll a few feet down the trail.

Dan tripped and fell backwards into the brush.

"Take it easy there, cowboy," Chris suggested.

Dan clambered up out of the brush and helped Chris push and roll the log over the edge of the trail and into the brush below.

They were gasping for breath.

"I'm done," Dan said. "That's enough for me for today."

Chris nodded. "I wonder where the hell Alex is," he said.

"She'll be along. She probably just found a nice place to swim." Dan reassured him.

Chris shook his head. "She's pretty good about this stuff," he said. "Her sister got lost once and we all went crazy looking for her.

That was years ago, but Alex knows to get back on time."

He looked at his watch. It was now almost five. "I think I am going to look for her," he said.

Dan looked at the tree they had cut, and the tools lying around. But he didn't feel like being the only one to clean up and he told himself that it would be quicker if Alex and Chris helped.

"I'll go with you," he said.

They left everything in place and pushed through the brush to get to the second big log on the trail. Dan looked at it and decided it was slightly smaller than the one they had just finished. They could get through that tomorrow morning, and that would leave only brush to clear from there on.

He looked ahead to see Chris hopping off the tree and landing on the part of the trail that had been cleared by someone else. At least they wouldn't have to deal with the brush, he thought.

They chatted as they hiked down the trail, with Chris occasionally giving a shout out to Alex.

But after half an hour on the trail, they had seen no sign of Alex other than a few footprints in the dust, and Dan was beginning to worry that maybe they might pass her by.

The trail now paralleled the river, and at times ran nearly along the shore. Each time this happened, Chris took the opportunity to give a shout down the canyon for Alex. And each time he sounded a bit more peeved.

Dan could feel the tensions rise. He didn't want to be worried about Alex, but the only other explanation was that she had ignored the time. He decided he would worry about her, and let Chris get angry. They'd shared the work up to this point, and there was no reason to change.

Dan tried to remember what Alex had been wearing. Black

leggings, and maybe a blue or purple top? No orange or red, colors that would more easily stand out in the canyon.

They stopped again near the river for Chris to yell.

chapter 29

On the far side of the river, a side canyon came down, and they soon saw Jackass Creek cascading down into the main river.

"The trail is on the west side of the creek," Chris pointed. "It goes up through that."

Dan saw only massive amounts of huckleberry oak. "That's a mess," he said. "Didn't you say you hiked down that?"

Chris pointed to a faint scar on his leg below the knee. "See that? All part of the fun."

He turned towards the canyon and gave another shout for Alex.

From here the trail was less obvious. No longer wending its way through brush and trees, it now led them out into a maze of granite slabs, boulders, and ledges.

Chris stopped and stared at the granite ahead, looking for a route.

Dan glanced down at the ground in front of the rock. "Looks like she came this way," he said, pointing to a boot print in the dust.

Chris quickly checked the footprint, then launched himself up the rock. "That's a good sign, I guess," he said. There was no corresponding print pointing the other direction.

But the route through the granite wasn't so clear. Solid slabs hid any footprints, and there were several routes that might work through the rock. And just to make things more complicated, every once in a while they would run across a cairn, but none of them seemed to be connected to each other, or a more likely route.

Since they didn't know which way Alex might have gone, at times they split up, Chris taking a route closer to the river, while Dan checked out the area further up in the rocks. And they took turns now, calling for Alex as they scrambled through the rocks.

Dan's route took him high above the water. At one point his phone beeped. It showed a text message from Kristen. "Call Cal ASAP. Urgent."

Dan chuckled. Urgent would have to wait until tomorrow afternoon, when they finally got out of this canyon. He turned back to finding a way through the blackened rock.

After a few hundred yards of starts and stops, Dan came to a large fissure in the granite that blocked his path. He turned back towards the river and began to edge his way down to Chris.

The fissure was deep, and he soon discovered Chris standing above it as well.

"Hard to see a way past this," Chris said.

The fissure was twenty to thirty feet deep, with sheer walls.

"It gets steeper up above," Dan told him.

Chris responded by giving another shout for Alex.

There was no answer, but Dan noticed something blue up in the trees on the far side of the river.

"What the hell is that?" he asked, pointing it out to Chris.

Chris shook his head.

They both looked down at the river, looking for a way off the granite.

Dan was first, heading back upstream along a ledge that took him down to the water. Chris was more direct, sliding down a slab to land on the rocks on the bank.

Now they began picking out a route over the boulders in the river to rock hop to the other side. Dan, with his long legs, was first across.

The blue was an old tarp, strung up in a grove of trees. There were a few rough-hewn poles stuck in the ground, and what looked like a clothesline or a line to tie up horses on the far side.

In the middle of the grove there were boards that were set up to form a wall, and the tarp had obviously been used as the roof.

"It's an old cowboy camp," Chris said.

Dan picked up an empty tin, the label identifying it as sardines still barely legible. "Doesn't look like this has been used for a while," he said.

Chris was poking around in the campfire ring nearby. He pulled out a couple of aluminum drink cans. "Probably people who were kayaking down here in the spring runoff," he said.

They took another look around the camp. Dan didn't see any footprints and said as much to Chris.

"She must be further down the canyon," Chris said. And this time, he didn't sound angry at all. He just sounded worried.

"Or she came over to this side of the river, and somehow we missed her," Dan suggested.

Chris rubbed at the back of his neck, then gave a huge sigh. "Yeah, I guess that's possible. But if she's not, then where is she?"

"How much farther could she have gone?" Dan asked. "Another mile? Two?"

Chris considered this. "I mean, if Alex is back at camp, then I could spend God knows how many hours down there looking for her. And she won't be there."

Dan checked his watch. "What if we keep going for another hour? That's about how far she could have got before she turned around. And then we still get back to camp before dark."

"That's going to make for a long day and a late dinner." Chris said.

"Tell you what," Dan suggested. "You keep going downstream and make sure she's not down there. I'll go back to camp and see if she's there. And I can get dinner ready for you when you get back."

"Yeah. Thanks." Chris was still staring down the canyon. "Shit."

"Well, one way or the other, she's around. Let's go find her," Dan said.

"Okay," Chris said. "See you back at the camp."

chapter 30

Dan watched Chris head down the canyon and then turned around to find a way back up the river.

He thought about trying to stay on the south side of the river on the way back to camp, but then remembered the footprints they had seen. He checked around for any dirt to see if there were footprints on this side, but gave up after a few minutes. There were no traces that he could see, other than his own prints, and Chris'.

He slipped his day pack over one shoulder and rock hopped back across the river.

Should he take the higher route, or the lower one through the granite? Dan decided to see if there were a middle route that might be possible.

He hoisted himself up over a ledge and took a quick look around. A cairn sat on a rock above him, and he scrambled up to it. From there he stopped and looked for more.

Fifty feet away, there was a small pile of three rocks. Was that a cairn that had fallen down? Maybe. But it would be hard to get to it. He chose a route that took him parallel to the river but below the little pile of rocks.

That worked for fifty feet before he found himself above a ten-foot cliff. To the left, he could see a set of boulders that could take him down, and carefully picked his way to the bottom, at one point turning around to face the cliff to make the climbing easier.

Another cairn, this one more obvious, led him forward up a slope. At the top he found himself on a narrow ridge that led up the canyon for a hundred feet or more, and he followed it up towards an ancient and gnarled juniper. If nothing else, the juniper was a good landmark here, just in case he needed one to help him remember the way back.

On the far side of the juniper was another cliff, this one even taller, although it seemed to have a few routes that might work to get past it.

Dan swore quietly to himself. He looked back down the ridge he had just walked up and considered going back down the river and starting again. That seemed like too much trouble.

He realized that he must be getting tired or dehydrated because he was being indecisive. He pulled out his water bottle and took a couple of long pulls on it. The water was still cold from the river, and tasted like heaven.

To his left the cliff looked as if it might get easier, and he explored a bit along the edge, looking for a way down.

That's when he saw the wrapper—a bright piece of foil at the base of the cliff. The sparkle of it caught his eye.

It's always easier to climb up something than to climb down it, but Dan eased himself over the edge of the cliff and slowly began to feel his way down to the bottom. Halfway down he realized that he was stuck. He couldn't find a good place to put either of his feet. He looked back up the cliff and considered climbing back up again. Then he looked down. It was still about six feet to the ground and the wrapper. Too far to jump without the possibility of an injury, at least at his age, and as tired as he was. And an injury here would be really bad news.

Instead of going down, Dan tried edging his way to the right, where he could see a crack in the rock. As his feet found the crack Dan found himself wishing for rock climbing shoes instead of his hiking boots. He jammed one foot into the crack and tested it.

It seemed good. Then he eased down, feeling with his hands for lower holds, and once he settled into those, he began to feel for the crack with his left foot.

A nub. That was all it was. A small bump in the rock, but it was better than nothing. Dan slowly shifted his weight, putting more of it on the nub, and decided he could trust it—at least with his hands still holding firm.

He gently eased his right foot out of the crack and reached it down the rock.

Nothing. Dan tried to see what was below. It looked like there was a small ledge, just out of his reach. He tried again, pointing his right toe, but still couldn't quite get there.

His hands were tiring now, and when his left foot slipped, Dan felt himself falling, sliding down the face of the granite, scraping the skin off both his hands.

And then his right foot caught on the ledge.

He stopped. The adrenaline rush was more than he expected. But now he was only three feet above the ground. He carefully launched himself off the rock and landed on the ground, flexing his knees to cushion the blow, and then rolling over backwards to use up some of the momentum.

It wasn't pretty. But he was down on the sand and pine needles at the base of the cliff. And he was only a few feet from the wrapper.

Dan picked it up. He noticed that the palm of his hand was bleeding.

But he also noticed that the wrapper was from an energy bar. In fact, it was exactly the kind of bar that had been stolen from his bear canister the last time he had come down the canyon.

It didn't take him long to make a decision. He scanned the cliff from below and found an easier way up this time.

There was no point in going back to the camp now. The wrapper wasn't his. Not on this trip. And it wasn't Chris' or Alex's, not with their all-natural food philosophy. That meant someone else. And if there was someone else down in this canyon, Chris might need all the help he could get.

And that meant Dan.

chapter 31

The trip back down to the river surprised Dan because it was so much quicker than his hike up. Of course, he now knew where he wanted to go, and knew the route to get there. That made all the difference. He made a quick mental note about the juniper and the small pile of rocks. And he even gave a nod to that first cairn.

Back at the river, he was on unfamiliar ground. He knew Chris started out on the other side of the river, but it seemed as if Chris was heading back to the river when he left Dan. Dan decided to stay on this side, both in the hopes he was following Chris' route, and also possibly Alex's.

And while Chris may have been taking his time, calling out for Alex, Dan was trying to make up for lost ground. He figured that if he got close enough to Chris he would hear his calls for Alex.

As he moved over the granite, he began to feel his breath shorten. It was still warm enough in the canyon that Dan was sweating now. And the light breeze of earlier in the afternoon seemed to have died. He was panting in the heat.

After one last jumble of rocks, the granite ridge petered out, and Dan found himself back in the open forest of the lower canyon. The trail was there, a dusty track weaving through the trees. Maybe that was why he couldn't hear Chris. The trees would absorb a lot of sound.

Dan checked for footprints, and quickly picked out Chris' distinctive swirling pattern. Those smaller ones were clearly Alex's. And he couldn't be sure, but it looked like there might be another set, but it was hard to tell if they were going up or down the canyon. Some of those prints seemed to be going in both directions.

He was now a few hundred feet from the river, and he considered going off trail to it to get some water. But he decided that could wait.

Instead, he followed the trail up and over a smaller granite knob. Here the trail was in decomposed granite, larger chunks than sand, and the footprints were much less distinct.

At the top of the knob Dan lost the trail. He checked back towards the river, and only found a single cairn. As he followed that, it led to a small campsite on a ledge above the river. Dan noted the fire ring and an obvious flat area for a tent, but the site hadn't been used for a long time. And there was no trail beyond the campsite. It overlooked a series of pools in a gorge. Perfect for fishing.

But there was nowhere to go from here.

Dan hiked back up the knob and looked straight down the canyon. He wasn't sure, but he thought he might have heard human voices. Was it Chris, yelling? He couldn't be sure. Not for the first time, Dan noticed how the noise of a river could sound like human voices, even when none were there.

He turned around to face the upper canyon, and that was where he noticed a faint track through the carpet of manzanita. It led away from the river, and down into a small brush filled arroyo.

Dan hopped down off the knob and explored the arroyo. The trail had clearly been run through here years and years ago. He could see there were clean cuts at the base of some of the buckthorn bushes that now had overgrown the trail, cuts that had been made a generation ago.

But underneath those bushes he saw the unmistakable tread of the trail, at times three feet wide, and leading downhill.

Dan pushed through the brush, this time noting that at least one of the branches across the trail had been broken recently. While it could have been done by a deer, he chose to believe that it showed that Chris had come this way.

It was a hundred yards of miserable bushwhacking down the arroyo. At times he couldn't see where he was placing his feet because the brush was so thick. And once he found himself falling into the empty bed of the creek at the bottom of the arroyo as he missed the trail. He eventually found it, as it had turned sharply to the left.

But at the bottom of the arroyo Dan could hear the river clearly. And as he pushed forward, he could see the white granite boulders, washed by the river that lined its shore.

At the base of a huge pine, Dan stopped to look around. The river was just off to his left, and as he looked at the ground near it, he could see Chris' footprints in the sand. That was where he could have gone to call out for Alex. He pulled out his water bottle and took another swig, leaving only a few ounces left. Then he looked at the river and drank the rest of the water. If he needed more, he knew where he could get it. He would worry about filtration later.

To his right, the bottom of the arroyo still held a trickle of water, and Dan could see the trail leading over to it. He followed it past a few trees, still not crossing the little creek. And then he came to the crossing. Someone, years ago, had done some real work on this crossing. The stones were huge and let Dan cross with just three large strides.

On the far side of the arroyo the trail led back up into a dense thicket of huckleberry oak. Dan swore quietly and started the climb up into the brush. He noted that someone had come this way recently. In the moist soil near the bottom of the arroyo they had slipped, leaving a clear slide mark in the damp dirt.

He stepped carefully through that section, hoping to avoid the same fate, and pushed up into the thicket of oak.

The brush was higher than his head here, and Dan couldn't help thinking that this was exactly the kind of place that wildlife liked to hide. He was sure, between his grunting and swearing, that he was making enough noise to scare it all aware.

In a small clearing he stopped to take a break. There were three trails that met in the clearing, but to Dan's eye one of them was obviously a deer trail. He chose the larger one leading downhill and plunged into the brush again.

As he pushed on, the branches dragged on his clothes, and he caught his leg on a particularly sharp branch that stopped him dead.

He began to wriggle his leg, straining his torso to see exactly where he was caught.

And that's when he heard the gunshot.

chapter 32

The gunshot stopped Dan cold.

He took a quick look around. Upstream, the thick brush led back to the arroyo and the river. But the gunshot came from down the canyon.

How far down? Not far, Dan guessed. A quarter of a mile? Half a mile? The rock of the canyon wouldn't absorb much of the noise, so it might have been farther away. But it sounded too damned close.

He finally wriggled his leg free and began to push through the brush in that direction. In the dense brush he couldn't see where he was going. He tried to balance the need to move quietly, to keep his presence hidden, with the need to move down the canyon quickly to help Chris.

There was no way to win that one.

Slowly he began to emerge from the brush into a more open forest. Now he really did have to move more carefully. Up ahead he could see the white rocks of the river, glowing faintly golden in the afternoon sunlight through the trees.

He pushed forward, trying to take cover behind the trees as he passed through them, his eyes roving from side to side, trying to pick up a clue, to detect some motion.

From ahead Dan heard a voice. Was it Chris? He couldn't make out the words, but the tone was angry, or anxious. It was strained.

Dan hurried forward, now with just a few trees between him and the open rocky banks of the river. The contrast between the dark of the forest and the bright sunlight of the river rocks made it hard for him to see ahead.

Again he heard the voice; this time it was closer. It was Chris.

Through the trees, the rocks in the river began to take shape. A few large blocks of granite stood between Dan and the river. And behind one of them Dan could see a shape. He paused for a moment, and then saw the shape move. It was a body, slumped on the ground.

It was Chris.

Dan raced forward and knelt down beside the fallen ranger. Chris' left side was covered in blood.

"What the hell happened?" Dan asked him.

"Fucker shot me," Chris replied, trying to show Dan his arm.

"Who?" Dan asked. "Where is he?"

Chris motioned with his chin. "Across the river," he said. "He's got Alex."

Dan glanced up. A shiver of terror shot through him. From where he was behind the boulder, he couldn't see much. As he started to stand up, Chris grabbed his arm.

"He'll shoot you," Chris said. The urgent tone, as much as the words, or Chris's weak grip on his arm, stopped Dan.

Dan looked again at Chris. Even in the warm light, Chris' face looked pale. Dan gently rolled Chris over onto his back and looked more carefully at his left arm. The shirt was soaked in blood, and Chris was not doing a very successful job of stanching the flow.

"Shit," Dan said. "We need to do something about your arm."

He pulled off his backpack and tried to remember what was in his first aid kit. Not much, as he recalled. It was just a small kit for a day pack. Dan tore it open and found a few gauze bandages and some antiseptic wipes.

Chris tried to stop him. "Don't worry about this," Chris urged him. "I'm fine. Go help Alex."

Dan was afraid that if he left Chris alone, the ranger might die from blood loss.

"A few seconds," he said. "We're just going to see what's going on here and stop the bleeding."

Dan cut off the sleeve of Chris' shirt, grateful for the sharp but tiny knife he carried in the day pack. The wound had left a large hole in Chris's arm. Dan quickly cleaned it up, using all of the materials in his first aid kit.

The wound still bled over Chris' shirt, and Dan took a bandage and his bandanna and wrapped them tightly around Chris' arm. It seemed to help.

"Okay, okay," Chris muttered. "That's good. Go help Alex."

Dan nodded. "Where is she?"

"On the far side of the river," Chris said. "There are some trees and a couple of big boulders. They're in the boulders." He paused to take a breath.

Just as Dan started to move, Chris grabbed him again with his good arm. "He's got Alex," Chris said. "And a rifle. Be careful."

"Yeah," Dan agreed. "Good idea."

"Don't leave Alex," Chris said.

"No," Dan promised him. "I won't."

As Dan slowly crept along the base of the rocks, he heard voices from the other side of the river. A man's voice, yelling. And a woman's voice, screaming.

He looked at Chris, whose eyes were wide in alarm.

Dan held up his hand. "I got this," he said to Chris. But he didn't believe it. Not for a second. Not against a guy with a rifle.

chapter 33

As he crept closer to the river, Dan heard Chris' voice again behind him.

"Do you see them?" Chris asked.

Dan shook his head, not knowing if Chris would see. He eased his tall body down between two rocks, and his feet hit the sand of the riverbed. To his left there were a series of rocks that led out across the stream, but they were completely exposed.

It was time to take a look. Dan moved back just a bit, so that his head might be partially hidden by a tiny bush growing out of the rocks, and peered over the top of the rock.

Chris had mentioned trees, but there were trees all over the south side of the river. Then Dan saw the two big boulders in between the trees—massive boulders that had fallen down from the cliffs above probably thousands of years ago.

The gap between the rocks wasn't large, and Dan couldn't quite see in between them. That, he realized, was a good thing. If he couldn't see inside, then it was just possible that whoever was inside couldn't see him.

He took another look at the rocks in the river. He wouldn't get a second chance at this one. If he fell, the splash would alert everyone. Even if he didn't fall into the river, the rocks were very exposed. He prayed they were all stable, that none would shift under his weight.

He needed to get across quickly. And he needed a place to hide on the other side.

It was like a chess match: Dan against the river. He had to pick the best route, the best rocks. And he had to get not only across the river, but over to that log on the left that might give him a tiny bit of cover once across.

Dan edged out from behind the boulder. The first rock was only three feet away. But it was completely out in the open. If he was going to be discovered, it would be now.

He took a deep breath, and took a moment to center his balance.

An angry scream from the far side of the river sent a sudden shot of adrenaline through him, and he strode out onto the first rock, and then the second, his brain and body racing at full focus. He couldn't stop to catch his balance. Instead, he used each step to re-center himself and launch himself toward the next stop in the chain of rocks. Step to step to rock to rock to rock. But do not stop.

There were more than he could count. Not six. Maybe ten or even twelve. He couldn't look that far ahead. All of his attention had to be on the next steppingstone in the series. This one was too tall, and nearly stopped him, but he bent his knee and quickly slid over to the lower one just past it. He kept moving.

He didn't dare look up, away from the next rock, but he was aware that the far shore was closer, much closer.

Two more steps, one more rock, and he was there.

He collapsed behind the log, facing back towards the river, and tried to catch his breath. His ears strained to hear any noise beyond the gentle sounds of the water in the river.

Nothing. That was a good sign, he hoped.

Dan rolled onto his stomach and crawled in the mud near the river towards the end of the log. A small mountain ash stood there, and he slowly crept into position behind it.

"Fuck you!" he heard Alex scream.

And his stomach turned when he heard someone laugh in response.

"Hey!" Dan heard Chris call from the far side of the river. "Let her go!"

The noises from his side of the river stopped, and Dan watched as a rifle barrel, and then a man came out from between the huge boulders. Thin, well under six feet, Dan decided. Dark hair, dark eyes, but underneath the red of the sunburn was pale skin. Blue jeans and a plaid shirt with the sleeves cut off. And a rifle. Something bigger than just a 22.

"Get the fuck out of here, or I'll kill her!" the guy yelled.

As Dan watched, the man scanned the far side of the river, looking for Chris.

"I can't leave!" Chris said. "She's my daughter."

"Tough shit," the man replied. "I'll kill her and I'll kill you. I don't care." He raised the rifle and fired off a shot towards the far bank, without aiming.

A warning shot. The sound exploded in echoes around the granite.

Dan wondered how many rounds the rifle could fire. Would he have to reload now? But the man didn't reload. He stood just outside the rocks and stared toward Chris.

When he got no answer, and saw no movement, he slowly walked back up into the slot between the rocks.

Dan considered his position. He was a good hundred and fifty feet from the rocks where Alex was being held. And in those hundred and fifty feet were a few trees, mainly on the uphill side, away from the river.

The ground here was mainly soft duff. It was damp down by the river, but further up by the trees it dried out.

Dan mentally charted a path towards the rocks. The first few feet would be in the open, but then he might be able to pick his way, hiding behind some of the huge pines, to within thirty or forty feet of the rocks.

But at that point, there were no trees for cover.

Dan decided he would cross that bridge when he got to it.

Slowly moving from the ground to a crouch, he held his breath and crept towards the first tree.

chapter 34

Dan had no plan.

This, he realized, was a serious problem. From behind the tree, he could see the jumble of rocks where he had to go. It was at least a hundred feet away. And while there were three trees that might provide cover on the way, that last forty feet was across open ground.

And he had no plan for crossing that.

At the same time, he couldn't wait behind the tree forever. The sounds coming from the boulders told him that a fierce struggle was under way. He needed to act.

On the ground at his feet Dan saw a few tired old pinecones. Nothing he could use as a weapon. As he searched the area, he also took note of the small branches there. Nothing was big enough to use as a club, but certainly large enough to snap under his weight and give his position away if he weren't careful.

And that was just what he could see on top of the pine needle duff. Who knew what was underneath, and might give him away just as effectively? The sound of the river would only cover up so much.

Too late, he realized that he should have grabbed a rock from near the river. But going back now would only make it more likely that he would be discovered. That was too big a risk to run.

Dan set his sights on the next tree, some fifteen feet away. He would have preferred to go on the uphill side of the tree he was hiding behind, but a few mountain misery bushes there close to the trunk made him fear it would make too much noise. And any noise would be too much at this point.

He stepped out gingerly from behind the tree and took first one, and then two steps ahead. Gently easing his weight from one foot to the other, he tried to move both quickly and silently to the next big tree. For a moment he was afraid he was losing his balance, and he struggled to stay upright. He shoved forward with one foot and tiptoed up to the tree.

A Jeffrey pine, he noted, somewhere in the back of his mind. The vanilla smell was unmistakable.

Once behind the tree, he glanced up across the river towards Chris. He could see the rocks from where he was, but there was no sign of movement up there. He prayed Chris was still alive. And staying out of the line of fire.

He had to keep moving.

The next tree was a bit further, maybe twenty feet, and he noticed now that the mountain misery around its base was thick. He would have to find a spot to hide behind the tree without crushing into that.

Again, he slipped his foot forward on the pine needles, his heart racing beyond anything he had ever experienced. He was afraid to breathe, both for fear it would give him away, and because he was trying so hard to hear any noises coming from the rocks ahead. He kept his mouth open, trying to hide the sound of his breath.

This time the steps took longer, and at least of one them snapped a small branch deep beneath the duff, a dull click as he moved.

He dived behind the tree, gasping for air, and waited, hoping that the noise had not been loud enough to reach the gunman by the rocks.

There was one more tree—this one a good thirty feet ahead of him. But here the ground had fewer needles. Dan could see a rough pattern of foot traffic now off to his right nearer the river, and if he could reach that, the ground was almost clear. It would allow him to walk silently.

But it would also leave him completely exposed.

He stuck to the hillside, slowly slipping one foot in front the other. It seemed excruciatingly slow, but he finally eased behind the last tree. He was getting better at this. A few more trees, and he would be really good at it.

But he didn't have any more trees. He didn't have any cover at all.

From the rocks ahead he could hear grunts of struggle and pain. He wondered if they would be enough to cover his approach.

Dan quickly calculated how long it would take him to cover the remaining fifty feet of open ground.

Three seconds? Four? And how long would it take the gunman to notice him, and aim and fire? Probably less.

If he were discovered right now, he would be dead.

Taking a deep breath, slowly exhaling through his open mouth so as not to make any noise, Dan settled his nerves for a few seconds, then slowly began to creep out from behind the last tree.

Each step took him closer to the rocks and Alex.

Once he got there? Dan was counting on surprise as his primary weapon. Enough surprise to create a diversion and let Alex escape. And then he would have to see what happened next. It wasn't much of a plan.

Another three steps. Forty feet to go. Still too far, probably, for a sprint.

Two more steps. Dan began to steel himself for a rush to the rocks. He glanced down at his feet to make sure there were no sticks to give him away. The ground was clear.

And when he looked up, he was face to face with a nasty-looking man with a rifle pointed right at his chest.

chapter 35

The first thought that went through Dan's mind was one of utter surprise. Who would have guessed that this was how he would die? Dan felt as if his head were slowly rising up out of his body, watching the whole scene from afar.

"I told you I was gonna kill you," the man said.

Dan slowly raised his arms. His brain was acting on its own, as if he didn't have any control. He wasn't sure if he was breathing or not. He wasn't sure if it mattered.

"Let her go," he heard himself say. "She's just a kid."

The gunman slowly raised the rifle to point at Dan's head.

"Get down on your knees," he said to Dan.

Dan felt his legs buckle for an instant. His brain kept assuring him that none of this could be happening. His eyes flickered back to the rocks, but the gunman blocked his view. Maybe Alex could escape if Dan did something. But there was nothing to do.

The rifle pointed at his head. And the gunman was now sighting it in.

"I said 'Get down on your knees.'"   This time the voice was tense and insistent.

Dan had time to confirm that there was no place for him to hide. There was no escape. Again he was surprised that his most powerful emotion seemed to be disappointment, and a sense that he was observing all of this from afar.

Dan straightened up and looked the gunman in the face. He didn't feel brave, just suddenly tired.

"No. I'm not going to do that," Dan said, shaking his head. "If you shoot me, you are going to have to do it while I'm standing here looking at you."

The gunman gave a derisive snort and leaned into the gun.

From behind him, Dan heard a yell. It was Chris.

"Let him go.' Chris yelled. "She's my daughter, not his."

The gunman's eyes flickered towards Chris, and he lowered the rifle just a bit.

"Let him go," Chris repeated, more desperately now.

A flash of adrenaline raced through Dan. Could he take advantage of the interruption and quickly overcome the gunman? But it was too late. If Chris was trying to create a distraction, Dan had not moved quickly enough. Or his nerve had failed him.

The moment of surprise was over, both for Dan and the gunman.

The rifle came back up again, pointing at Dan's head.

"I'll kill you," the man said quietly. "And then I'll kill him."

It took forever.

At least, it seemed that way to Dan. This is what it is like to die, Dan thought. Pretty painless, at least. His brain made a quick search of the rest of his life. Any regrets? He sent a short telepathic apology to Kristen, assuring her that he wished things hadn't ended this way.

His eyes were swimming in a strange sea: his body seemed to float away, disconnected from anything that was happening here.

The gunman's head was now floating in front of Dan, the long barrel of the rifle seeming to reach out towards Dan, almost touching him.

"No!" Dan heard Chris scream.

Dan could see the man's finger on the trigger of the rifle. He could see it tighten. Dan began to feel faint, and he wobbled just a bit on his feet. Behind the head of the gunman a strange black blob began to materialize, floating behind him like some kind of tiny black cloud of death.

Dan closed his eyes.

The noise was not what Dan expected. A dull metallic boom, then followed by the explosion of the rifle firing. The noise was deafening.

And then time stopped still, and his world went black.

It took a second for Dan to realize that he was not dead. His ears were ringing with the echoes of the explosion. That was a good sign.

He didn't feel any pain. That was another good sign.

He opened his eyes to a startling scene. The gunman had been transformed. His outer body fallen in a heap on the ground. And in its place was a small, witch-like creature whose clothes were in shreds. She was screaming.

Dan realized it was Alex.

The gunman lay at her feet with the rifle underneath him at an odd angle.

His adrenaline now fully engaged, Dan staggered, leapt and then raced forward. Alex raised her hand again, holding a cast iron skillet high over her head. She stepped forward and stumbled, her feet tripping over the legs of the gunman. The skillet came down in a crazy, swinging arc that missed its main target and struck the man's back with a metallic thud.

Dan threw himself at the gunman, flying on top of him and landing hard with a heavy thump. He heard a crack underneath him, and wondered if it was a bone, or a stick underneath them both. He decided he didn't care.

Dan spun around on top of the gunman and yanked the man's arms back away from the rifle. He heard a scream and was happy to know that this time it came from the gunman, not from Alex.

He pinned the man's arms tightly behind him and yelled for Alex to get the gun.

But Alex wasn't listening.

As Dan looked up, he saw her face contorted with rage, her whole body shaking.

"You fucker!" she screamed. And then, pulling her leg back and grimacing with fury, she kicked the man as hard as she could in the groin. "Fuck you!" she punctuated the kick with another yell.

The man under Dan gave a hideous groan, his entire body reacting to the kick.

"Alex!" Dan yelled. And then, slowly and firmly, "Get. The. Gun."

This time Alex might have heard him.

Gasping for breath she stopped and looked at Dan. Slowly his words sank in.

Alex bent over to pick up the rifle, staring the whole time at the gunman's face. As she took it in her hands, she pursed her lips and spit right into the gunman's face.

Dan looked around for help. He couldn't hold the gunman's arms forever.

Alex flung the rifle behind her, still staring at the man.

Dan watched as she gathered herself together, then prepared to aim another kick at him.

"Alex!" Dan yelled again. "I've got him. Get some rope."

Alex stepped back and looked at Dan again.

He pointed to the rocks with his chin. "Go see if there is some rope in there," he said.

She didn't want to go. Dan could see that she wanted to kick the man again. Maybe many times.

"Rope," he said to her quietly. "Go get some rope, Alex."

Without a word Alex turned and walked towards the rocks.

Dan turned from her to look at the gunman. He could see only one side of the man's face, but it was contorted with pain. He was crying, tears pouring out.

Dan tightened his grip on the man's arms, and the man gave another whimper of pain.

Dan looked up towards the rocks where Chris had been. He thought he saw Chris' head above the rocks, but he couldn't be sure.

"Chris!" Dan yelled.

Yep, that was his head. Chris waved an arm to signal, then disappeared again behind the rock.

Dan checked his grip on the gunman. The man's left arm was at an odd angle, and Dan realized that something about it wasn't right. Broken? Or the collar bone?

Alex returned with a long piece of nylon rope. She stood in front of Dan, in front of the gunman, and held out the rope to Dan.

Dan shook his head at her.

"Tie his feet together," Dan instructed Alex. "Do you know how to tie a good knot?"

Alex stared again at the gunman. For a moment, Dan thought she was going to kick him again. Instead, she dropped to her knees and quickly tied the rope around the gunman's feet.

First a simple and tight loop around each ankle, then a large loop around them both.

She looked at Dan. He nodded.

"Get a knife, and cut off the rest of the rope," Dan told her.

Again, Alex went back into the rocks. This time she came out with a large hunting knife.

Just for a second, Dan worried that she was going to stab their captive.

But Alex knelt by his feet and sliced through the rope.

"Good," Dan said.

As Alex stood up, Dan directed her to pick up the rifle.

He looked down at the gunman. There was clearly something wrong with his right shoulder.

Dan leaned over to talk to him.

"I am going to let go of your arms so that you can move them in front of you," he said. "When I do that, you will move very slowly. Anything funny, and I will grab this arm," and here he gave a little tug to the man's left arm, happy to see the man flinch, "and I will yank it so hard that you will wish it was gone."

The man nodded slightly to show Dan that he understood.

Dan straddled the gunman and gently turned him over onto his back. The man gingerly moved his left arm, contorting his whole body to bring it out on his chest, where he held it with his right arm. He gave a groan of pain and settled into place.

Dan took the rest of the rope from Alex and quickly tied the man's hands together as they crossed on his stomach.

"Don't move, and it won't hurt so much," Dan told him. But from the look on the man's face, he already knew this.

Dan sat up, taking his weight off the man, and looked around.

Now what?

chapter 37

Alex came back into Dan's field of vision. She leaned over and looked at the man's face.

"You fucker," she started again.

Dan was afraid she was going to attack the guy again.

"Alex," he said. "Go see about your dad."

She stopped and looked at him.

"Go take care of your dad," Dan repeated. "He's hurt. Up there in those rocks." He pointed vaguely in Chris' direction.

Suddenly, Alex looked down at herself. Her clothes were torn nearly off her body, and large areas of bare flesh were exposed. She quickly turned around to face away from Dan.

Dan looked down at his prisoner. The man appeared to be barely conscious.

Dan stood up and took quickly took off his shirt.

"Here," he said to Alex, and reached in front of her to hold the shirt out for her to see.

She stared at the shirt for a moment, then quietly took it and slipped it on. It was enormous on her, and she wrapped it around herself, holding it tight.

Dan pulled out the nylon belt from his pants and gave it to her.

This time she grabbed the belt and tied it around her waist.

She still wasn't looking at Dan.

"Go see your dad," he urged her. "He needs help."

Alex didn't say anything, but she started walking down to the river. Dan watched her go for a moment, then turned to check on the man on the ground.

Still no motion or activity. Dan wondered how hard Alex had hit him with the skillet. Hard enough for a concussion? That would add to his problems.

Dan didn't know how much medical training Alex had. He wondered if she would be able to help Chris at all, or if Chris would be able to give her advice. He thought about leaving the man here and going to see. But he had seen too many magic shows, where people escaped from this kind of thing all the time.

Admittedly, they weren't doing it with a broken collarbone, but still.

Dan decided that he couldn't take the chance.

He looked up again at the river. Alex was now across, climbing the boulders towards her father. She was going too far upriver.

"Alex," Dan yelled, "to your left!"

Alex turned around and stared at Dan for a moment, then adjusted her route up the rocks. Soon she appeared to jump forward, and she disappeared behind the granite. She had found Chris.

Dan looked around again. It was getting late in the day. The shadows in the canyon were beginning to reach out from the bottom of the cliffs to the west, putting more and more of the gorge in shade. He realized that he was shaking. He needed to sit down. But he didn't have time to waste.

He could see the shadows approaching through the trees behind him. It wouldn't take long for night to come.

How much daylight did they have left? Maybe an hour and a half? Two hours? And then maybe an hour of dusk.

It probably wasn't enough time to hike out to the trailhead, even if Chris could walk. Even if this idiot at his feet was willing to cooperate.

Back at the camp, they had three sleeping bags. Would he give his bag to the gunman? God, that would be awful. But he also couldn't leave the man alone at night without anything to keep him warm.

There must be a sleeping bag or blankets in the rocks. Maybe that would work. But one way or the other, Dan guessed that he wouldn't be getting much sleep tonight.

He hoped he could stay awake. The last thing he wanted was for this guy to get free.

He looked back up the rocks. There was still no sign of Alex.

Dan gave a glance over to the pile of rocks that hid the gunman's camp. Did he dare risk it?

He looked down. The guy seemed to be out for the count. Dan wondered again about a concussion, or worse.

Dan quietly eased away, towards the rock, always keeping an eye on his prisoner.

It was only ten feet. Maybe fifteen. And he was halfway there.

"Dan!" he heard Alex yell.

Dan spun around to look at the prisoner. The man was still lying quietly on the ground.

"Dan!" Alex yelled again. "Help!"

The situation had just gotten a lot worse.

chapter 38

It really wasn't much of a decision. Dan had to go help Alex and Chris and leave the gunman here on the ground.

He picked up the rifle and walked quickly back down to the river. From this side a new route appeared, and he began the process of picking his way over this rock and that, stepping up onto the large boulder, and then following that line of flat ones over there…

He had only two or three rocks to go when he heard yelling from up above. "Sheriff's Department! Drop the gun! Raise your hands! Get down on the ground! Get down on the ground!"

Dan was stunned. He looked up at the rocks to see two officers pointing their guns at him.

He tried to explain that he was a ranger with the forest service, but he couldn't get a word in edgewise. They were screaming now: "Drop the gun! Get on the ground! Raise your hands!"

Dan looked for a dry spot near the river and slowly began to lower the rifle to the ground. Over the voices of the officers he tried again to explain that he was on their side.

"I'm with the forest service," he said loudly. But they didn't hear him. They were too busy yelling for him to get down on the ground with his hands over his head.

The problem was that there was no place to do this. The rocks near the river were anything but flat, and Dan was worried that if he tried to move in any direction they would shoot.

He began to bend his knees, looking for a place to prostrate himself… and not finding it.

That was when he heard Alex's voice over the top of the deputies' shouts. "No! That's Dan," she said. "He's a ranger."

That got through.

There was a brief moment of silence, and then one of the deputies called out to him. "What's your name?"

Dan gave them his name and explained that he worked for the forest service with Chris, the guy who was wounded up there.

With both deputies continuing to aim their guns at Dan, one of them slowly approached and told Dan to keep his hands in the air.

"Are you armed?" he asked Dan when he was six feet away.

Dan considered mentioning that he wasn't even wearing a shirt but decided against it. "Just the rifle down there," he said. "And that's not mine."

"What about a knife?"

Dan pointed with his chin up to Chris and Alex. "In my daypack up there." He didn't mention that it had a tiny blade.

The officer told Dan to turn around slowly. Dan did, and the officer quickly frisked him cursorily, then told him to turn around again. With relief, Dan saw that he was holstering his weapon.

"What's going on here?" he asked Dan.

As concisely as he could, Dan explained that across the river was the owner of the gun, who had attacked and kidnapped Alex, and tried to kill Dan.

The officer's eyes traveled away from Dan, up towards the gunman. "So where is he now?" he asked.

Dan didn't want to turn around, away from the deputy. "Up there, under those trees, in front of the big rocks.

The deputy crouched down and pulled Dan down with him.

"Where, exactly?" he asked.

Dan looked up at where he had left the gunman. At first, he thought he was mistaken. Then he realized that the gunman had moved. And Dan didn't know where.

He pointed out the last known location of the gunman to the deputy.

"Is he armed?" the deputy asked.

"No idea," Dan admitted. "He had this rifle up in those rocks, but he could have more up there."

The sheriff crouched down a bit more. "Okay. You go up there and tell my partner what you just told me," he said. "I'll cover you from down here."

Dan took a deep breath and scanned the route up the rocks to where Alex, Chris, and the other deputy were. It was not an ideal route, and he would be out in the open for a lot of it. He hoped the deputy was as good as his word.

The deputy muttered a few words into a microphone on his shoulder and nodded to Dan. "Get going."

Dan picked his way quickly through the rocks. In less than a minute he dropped down behind the boulder where Chris and Alex were waiting with the deputy. Chris didn't look good. He was pale and it seemed to Dan that he had trouble keeping his eyes open. Maybe he was just resting. He did greet Dan with a weak smile before closing his eyes again.

While Dan caught his breath, he turned to the second deputy and brought him up to speed.

"Okay," the young man said. "You stay here with these two and wait for the chopper. And then you three get the hell out of here. I'm going to help the deputy down there," pointing to his partner.

"Where the hell did you guys come from?" Dan asked in amazement.

The deputy stopped and turned around. "We got a call from the Sheriff over in Tuolumne County about a most-wanted armed and dangerous fugitive, and some hikers in trouble," he said.

Dan was confused. "How did they know about it?" he asked.

The deputy waved him away. "Go meet the chopper," he said. "Get out of here."

"What chopper?" Dan asked. "Where?" He wondered just what the hell was going on. But the deputy just waved him off and continued down towards the river.

Dan felt someone tugging at his arm.

"They called it in on their radio GPS thingy," Alex said to him. "It's going to where we camped."

chapter 39

Dan turned and looked at Alex.

"Are you okay?" he asked her.

"I'm worried about my dad," she said, avoiding his question. "How are we going to get him up there?" Dan could tell she was having trouble controlling her tears. He could understand that perfectly.

Dan looked again at Chris and had to agree with Alex's assessment.

"The guys in the chopper can help," he said. "They're experts and they'll know exactly what to do."

Dan cast a quick look over the top of the rock. The two deputies were still on this side of the river, their focus and their guns aimed across at where Dan had left the gunman.

"I don't think we can carry your dad back to camp," Dan said to Alex. "So one of us should stay here with your dad and one should go back to camp to meet the chopper."

Alex took this in. She clearly didn't want to leave her father.

"Are you okay staying here with him?" Dan asked.

Alex nodded. Dan noticed that her eyes were tearing up.

"Okay," he said. "You stay here and take good care of him, and I'll get back to camp to meet the chopper."

Alex didn't answer.

"Hey," Dan said to her. "I'm sorry. I never said thank you. So, thank you."

Alex looked at him. "For what?" she asked.

"For saving my life," Dan said.

Alex looked away. "He said he would kill me if I didn't stay put," she said quietly.

"Yeah, but you didn't stay put," Dan said. "So, thank you."

Alex was still not meeting his gaze.

Dan reached out and put a hand on Alex's shoulder and waited for her to look at him. "Don't worry, Alex," he said. "Your dad will be okay. We'll get him out of here and get him safe."

He wasn't sure she believed him. He wasn't sure she even heard him.

He hoped he was telling her the truth. Then he ran up the trail and back to camp.

Before he could get there, he heard the chopper flying into the narrow slot of the canyon. He turned and looked up, to see it flying in low, just above the trees, and coming up the canyon like an oversized and deafening mechanical osprey.

Dan stopped at the top of a granite knoll above the trail and waved his arms at the chopper.

It was only a matter of seconds before he saw the men in the helicopter point to him and then wave. The machine was glittering in the sunlight above the shady part of the canyon.

The downdraft nearly knocked Dan down, and he dropped back from the top of the knoll. He could see the pilot looking around, trying to gauge the spot for a landing.

After only a few seconds, the chopper turned in place and slowly descended down towards the top of the knoll. In the side door Dan could see two men ready to jump out.

And then the chopper dropped lower and lower, and Dan had to cover his face and turn away. The blast from the rotors was overpowering. He tried to back away even more, but had a hard time seeing where he was going. After struggling for a few minutes, and making only minor progress, Dan stopped in a crouch. He heard a change in the chopper's engine, and then it was up and away down the canyon.

By the time Dan had recovered he was looking at two EMTs and a stretcher.

"Where are we going?" one of them yelled at him.

Dan pointed down the canyon. One of the medics handed Dan a backpack to carry. "Take this," he said. "Do you know where we're going?"

Dan nodded.

"Let's go!" the medic yelled.

Somehow, it took longer to get back to Alex and Chris than Dan had expected. And there were a few spots where the two guys with the stretcher struggled to get through. How the hell were they going to do that with Chris on the stretcher?

But at the bottom of the last steep section Dan broke into a trot through the trees, and quickly found his way to greet Alex.

"How's he doing?" he asked.

Alex didn't answer. She was holding Chris' hand and crying.

The medics arrived and quickly moved Alex and Dan out of the way. With impressive efficiency they took Chris' vital signs and made a series of decisions, hooking him up to an IV and giving him an injection.

Dan put his arm around Alex. She was shivering, even though it was still warm in the canyon.

Within a few minutes, the medics were ready to move Chris.

They explained the plan to Dan and Alex.

"Can you help?" one of them asked Dan. "We can use an extra pair of hands up there in the rocks."

Dan nodded.

"I can help, too," Alex offered.

The medic looked at her carefully. "Okay, good," he said. "Let's get going."

The two medics directed them as they gently lifted Chris onto the stretcher, and Dan pointed the way back up the trail. It was going to be a struggle.

Once into the rocks, it took time and hard work for them to maneuver the stretcher up between the boulders and over the slabs. Dan admired the way the medics gave clear, focused direction to him and Alex. And how Alex seemed to put her whole heart into every step, every move, even as she wiped away her tears. She was focused. He was amazed at how tough she was.

At one point one of the medics turned to Dan and asked him how much farther they had to go to get to where they had been dropped off.

Dan explained where the trail went, but he didn't know how long it would take them to get there with the stretcher.

The medic spoke into his radio, and within minutes Dan heard the chopper coming back.

As it hovered overhead, they brought the stretcher and Chris up to the top of the knoll.

Dan backed away, knowing what to expect from the chopper.

The medic looked at Dan. "You coming with us?" he asked.

Dan shook his head. "I think I'll stay here."

The medic looked at Alex. "What about her?" he asked Dan.

A look of panic raced across Alex's face.

"She needs to get out of here," Dan said. "She needs medical attention, too."

The medic nodded, then consulted with the pilot.

He turned around and held out his hand to Alex. "Let's go," he yelled.

And he pulled Alex into the chopper.

chapter 40

Once again Dan was left choking in a blistering tower of dust as the chopper took off. It soared off into the sky and within seconds it was out of sight, over the top of the canyon walls and away.

And then he was alone.

He thought about going to see if the deputies below needed any help but decided against it. They had told him to leave, and Dan wasn't sure exactly what an unarmed and shirtless man could do down there.

He looked around for his daypack. It had a rain shell in it, at least. Then he remembered Alex setting it down on the ground when they were struggling with the stretcher on the granite.

He hiked back down and found it, lying next to Chris,' and picked them both up. He noted with a grin that his seemed to be lighter, and opened Chris' to find two apples.

Suddenly aware of how tired, thirsty, and hungry he was, Dan gratefully bit into on one of the apples. The juice exploded in his mouth, and he sat down on the granite to enjoy the sensation. It was a damn good apple, so good that it brought tears to his eyes. At least, that was his story.

It was so good that Dan immediately decided to eat the second one as well, each bite a new surprise about how delicious an apple could be.

It occurred to him that maybe the apple tasted so good because he nearly died earlier that day, and he decided that maybe that was true. But the apples were still delicious. He would have to tell Chris.

He ate them down to the very nubs of the cores, then ate even the cores, swallowing the seeds. That left him with just the two tiny stems, which he tossed into the brush below him. That was one way to deal with your trash in the wilderness.

By the time he had picked apart the last apple, Dan was ready to get moving again. The sunlight was fading now, with sun only on the very tops of the cliffs above him. He had a tiny headlamp in his pack, but it was time to get back to camp.

The hike back left Dan's mind to wander. His body seemed to know where it was going and didn't need his attention. From below he could hear another helicopter and wondered what was going on down there. He worried about Chris, and about Alex. What had happened to her in those rocks? Had she been raped?

No question that she had saved his life. And in a way, he had rescued her. Not with the best plan, but still. They got out alive. That was the important thing. They all got out okay. That got him thinking about Chris again. He hoped they had all got out alive. The EMTs seemed confident. But that was their job, to seem confident and optimistic. It was all part of their bedside manner.

For the third time Dan tripped over a small bump in the trail and realized he was having trouble moving, his feet stumbling from time to time. A full day of trail work, followed by the rest of the day's experiences had left him completely exhausted.

He slowed down just a bit and tried to focus more on the trail. As he passed through the brush they had cleared earlier, he noted a couple of branches that he'd like to trim back and gave a short laugh. That was for another day.

At the huge log they had cut, he stopped and picked up as many tools as he could, hoisting the saw over his shoulder, tossing the wedges into his pack. At least the rest of the trail was clear from here on.

He came to the bottom of the final climb up a granite section and paused. It seemed steeper than he remembered it, and it took a real effort to put one foot in front of the other, lifting his body with each step.

Damn, he was tired.

On the other side, the trail dropped down into the clearing where the three of them had camped. Daylight was gone now, and only the matte glow of the sky above gave Dan enough light to see.

The camp was perfectly still. There were no shadows anymore, only darker areas beneath the trees where they had pitched their tents. The bats would be out soon, if they weren't already.

Dan reached his own tent and dropped his daypack. It clattered to the ground, reminding him of the wedges inside. He really needed to get something to eat. But first, he unzipped his tent and rummaged around for a shirt. With the sun gone down, it was cooling off, and he grabbed a fleece jacket and slipped it on.

That was better. It seemed to ease warmth into him.

He went over to the two bear canisters and opened up his. He wondered if Chris had something better to eat, but decided on his usual dinner of miso soup and a freeze-dried meal. Tonight what he had was lasagna.

He filled his cook pot with water and set it on the stove to boil. The dusk was deepening. Dan got up and went back to his pack and dug out his headlamp. It felt strange, being the only person in camp, wandering through it with the other gear set up around him.

It was getting darker now, and the blue flame of the stove

provided little light. He sat on a nearby log, resting his knees.

He shined the light down into the pot and was happy to see it was beginning to form a few bubbles on the bottom. Not long now.

Chris' tent over there. Alex's beyond that. Dan suddenly realized how quiet it was in camp. If there was noise from down in the canyon, it wasn't getting to him here. Or maybe the deputies had found the gunman and had choppered out of there. It was no longer his problem.

He sat back on the log and closed his eyes.

A slight noise brought him back to awareness, and he realized it was the sound of the water boiling in his pot. He poured some into a cup with his soup mix, and poured the rest into the pouch with his lasagna and stirred it.

He turned off the stove and sat back to sip the soup. The only sound now was the river, down below, continuing its rush down the canyon. Dan drank the soup and listened. There were no other noises. The birds were quiet. A flicker of motion overhead caught Dan's attention and he saw the first bat of the night, silently swirling through the trees after insects.

Dan watched for a while, then realized that his dinner was probably ready. He opened the pouch and checked. Not quite, but good enough. He ate straight from the pouch. No need to get a bowl dirty tonight. It was salty and not quite rehydrated and Dan didn't care.

It didn't taste great. Dan realized that he was probably too tired to know how hungry he really was. He finished off the lasagna quickly, then dug into his bear can for some dried mangoes and apricots. And something for dessert. Did he pack one more chocolate bar?

There it was. He could feel it with his fingers. He pulled it out and stared at it in the light of his headlamp. Chocolate hazelnut. His favorite. Dan decided that he would eat the whole thing—normally the bar would be good for at least two nights, maybe three.

And then it would be time to put away the food, brush his teeth, and get into bed. The rituals he knew by heart. Tonight they seemed to take longer than usual, as his mind wandered.

Around him, the forest was already asleep.

Dan climbed into his tent and within minutes was in his sleeping bag, his body slowly warming up the nylon lining. He lay there listening to the quiet sounds of the river. No other noises to hear.

Then, off on the other side of the river, the gentle hooting of an owl.

Dan closed his eyes and listened to the owl.

And fell into a deep sleep.

chapter 41

He woke up twice in the night. The first time he found himself struggling to get his feet free of the confines of his mummy bag, and his arms were flailing. It took him some time to settle his nerves from that and fall back asleep.

The next time he woke up it was nearly morning. The sky had just started to lighten perceptibly in the east, at the head of the canyon. Dan knew it would be at least an hour before the sun would hit the top of the ridges above him. And maybe another hour before it reached down into the bottom of the canyon itself.

He allowed himself to lie there, resting, not worrying about going back to sleep, but just enjoying the quiet, the subtle murmur of the river. The dawn chorus of birds would begin soon. He closed his eyes and let his ears take it all in.

The next thing he knew, it was morning in earnest, with the sun lighting up the canyon around him.

He climbed out of his bag and quickly slipped on his clothes. He hadn't figured out how he was going to deal with the two extra packs. He thought about that while he pulled on his boots.

He emptied out his bear can—the last two packets of oatmeal, the last packet of cocoa. As he hefted the bag of craisins he decided that he could go ahead and finish them as well, even though there were more than he would usually eat.

He set a pot of water to boil and began to stuff his sleeping bag into its sack. By the time he had it put away, and his pad deflated and rolled up, the water was boiling.

He sat on his log and ate his breakfast. The two other tents seemed lost, lonely. His thoughts drifted to Chris and Alex, and he sent them a little prayer. He munched a few walnuts with his oatmeal.

Breakfast finished; it was time to pack up. But he found it hard to concentrate, as if he were shell-shocked. He knew that he and Chris had planned to work at least the first half of the day, before hiking out. But what to do now? He could keep working on the trail, but rejected that idea. He was going home.

He took a few extra minutes to recover from it all and then decided it was time to load his pack. The sleeping bag in the bottom, with the pad. He put the rest of his clothes on the log, out of the dirt, and rolled up his tent. It was always a matter of pride for him to fit it neatly back into its stuff sack, better than it had arrived new. And a number of things went into the bear can, since it was empty of food. His folded clothes fit in around the larger items. That left him with a neat and tidy pack. The ritual of it all helped him settle his mind.

But now Dan decided he had to pack up the other two tents. He started with Chris' and opened the zipper. It felt vaguely like eavesdropping to stick his head into the tent. He took a quick inventory: sleeping bag, pad, some clothes, a book to read, and an extra pair of camp shoes—more than Dan would usually take on an overnight trip.

Dan bundled it all up and fitted the items one by one into Chris' pack. There was plenty of room because the pack was huge. And he had room in Chris' bear canister, too. It took a little more fitting and fiddling, but he soon had Chris' gear packed up.

He would deal with the tools later. He'd take as many as he could, either inside or tied to his pack. And carry the rest? He'd have to see how that felt.

Now it was time for Alex's tent. This really did feel like an invasion of privacy. He wondered what Alex would say if she saw him climbing into her tent, into her space and her things.

The sleeping bag and pad were easy. He put those away quickly. And then it was time to deal with the clothes. He found a small stuff sack and quickly pushed them all into the sack. Her pack was smaller and had just enough room for her gear. When he was done, he lifted it up. He guessed something like fifteen pounds, maybe a bit more. It would be easy to carry that one in addition to his own. He felt a pang in his heart for the pain she was feeling. That, and a slightly warm feeling that what he was doing would help, both her and Chris.

The sun was up now, and its warmth allowed Dan to slip off his fleece jacket and tie it onto to the top of his pack. He had everything ready for his hike out.

Except Dan wasn't ready. He walked down to the river to filter a bit more water, even though he didn't need it. There were too many thoughts racing around in his head, and he was in no hurry to get back to emails, text messages, and the rest of the world. He decided that he really didn't want to talk to anyone right now, or maybe ever.

As he stood down near the river, he was startled to hear noises from up the canyon. Voices, he was almost sure. This time it wasn't the river itself.

He turned and walked back to the campsite. Sure enough, a few minutes later a group of four men came hiking down the trail, chatting away. They stopped suddenly when they saw him.

"Who the hell are you?" one of them asked in amazement.

"Where are you going?" another asked.

Dan explained who he was and asked them what they were doing.

"Forensics," one of them answered. "Headed to the crime scene down here. Do you know where it is?" He was looking at Dan, while one of the other men was checking a GPS unit. A third man was talking into a walkie-talkie.

Dan pointed down the canyon. "A couple miles or more," he said.

"Were you down there yesterday?" another man asked. "What the hell happened?"

Dan thought about this for a minute. "You should ask the deputies down there," he said. "They know more than I do." He wasn't in the mood to relive the whole thing again.

After a brief consultation, the four men thanked Dan and continued on down the trail. But before they left, the guy on the walkie-talkie turned to him.

"They want you to stay here," he said to Dan. "Stay here and wait for the Sheriff."

Dan looked at his pack on the ground. It wouldn't be hard to ignore that direction.

Instead, he went back down to the river, took off his boots, and sat in the sand in the sun. That was where the Sheriff would find him.

chapter 42

It was a good hour and a half before a deputy from the Sheriff's office walked into Dan's camp and called out, "Hello?"

Dan got up to greet him and was surprised to see he wasn't one of the two men he had met yesterday. They must have choppered in more people at some point.

"You the ranger that was down there when all this happened?" the deputy asked.

Dan admitted that he was.

And was then asked to relive the whole thing from beginning to end.

With a deep breath, Dan began.

He was surprised at how hard it was to tell the story. Thinking about Chris and Alex made it hard for him to breathe, his throat tightening up. And while the deputy was patient and understanding, it didn't really help.

Dan tried to distract himself by asking the deputy about what had happened afterwards, when Dan had left the two officers in the canyon below. But the deputy told him that he didn't want to answer any of those questions until he'd heard Dan's report completely. Just to make sure Dan was telling only what he knew.

Dan sighed and started again. The deputy was recording everything, and about halfway through his account, Dan decided to get it all out of the way at once, and went back to the very beginning: the phone call, the conversations, the first trip down here, the rocks moved out of place, the missing loppers, the stolen food…everything that he could think of.

He had started with a simple chronological account, but by the time he was done he realized that he had meandered all over, cut and pasted from timeline to timeline, and left even himself slightly confused by it all. And he was exhausted.

The deputy had been taking notes the whole time, and then spent another half hour trying to put everything back into its place and time. Sometimes the same question got asked two or three times, and Dan tried to remember how it all fit together. Sometimes his answers didn't match, or the deputy had misunderstood, and they had to go over that part again.

When they were done the deputy thanked Dan, and Dan took a look at his watch. It was now nearly noon. He figured they had been at it for more than an hour and a half.

And he was really hungry.

He still had a little cheese and salami in his pack, and he remembered that Chris had food in his bear can—maybe more fruit. While the deputy reviewed his notes and checked in by walkie-talkie, Dan ate what food he had left.

That was when the deputy told him he was cleared to leave.

"What about these packs and tools?" Dan asked him. "Are these evidence?"

The deputy looked around and shook his head. "I don't think so," he said. "You can take them out of here."

Dan raised his eyebrows. "No, I can't," he said. "That's three packs and a bunch of tools, and I'm one guy. Any chance you guys could help the victims here by getting their gear back to them?"

He thought using the word "victim" was a good idea. Maybe it would help.

The deputy thought this over.

"Yeah, okay," he said. "If you can leave all this stuff in one place, right by the trail, I'll see if I can get a couple of the officers to help get it out of here."

"That would be great," Dan said with relief. He quickly piled all the gear closer to the trail, all lined up in a row so that nobody could miss it.

Dan hoisted on his pack. It felt light without the food in it. And he was only going to carry one bottle of water. He had lots more of that back at the truck.

He looked at the pile of tools and thought of taking off his pack and trying to fit more stuff into it, maybe a pair of loppers and the small saw. And he could carry the shovel in one hand, and Alex's pack in the other.

That would just leave Chris' pack, the McLeod, and the big saw. He considered trying to carry both the shovel and the McLeod over his shoulder with one arm and Alex's pack in the other. He stood there and felt the weight.

Then he put down everything but his own pack. He tightened the straps and belt, gave it a quick shrug with his shoulders, and started to hike back out to the trailhead.

Someone else could deal with the rest of that gear.

chapter 43

When Dan finally started hiking out of the canyon it was already after noon—his least favorite time to hike, in the heat of the day, and right after eating.

It wasn't the salami or cheese, but Dan had a lousy taste in his mouth. The pristine canyon he had worked to explore was now crawling with people—people who really didn't care about the silence, or the granite. Working people who were oblivious to the magic around them.

He found himself walking faster, harder. Up over the granite, through the manzanita. He had to admit that the extra foot traffic had begun to wear a pattern in the trail, making it easier to follow in those areas where he and Chris hadn't done much to improve it. The tree they had cut as a bridge already began to have signs of wear on it.

The thought of Chris gave his stomach a lurch, and he promised himself to call as soon as he could to check on the guy. And Alex. What a mess this whole trip had turned out to be.

The last mile of the trail ran in the trees high above the river, where he could see down into the deep pools between the boulders below. The water there was deeper than turquoise, turning almost black in the deepest sections shaded by the rocks. Those pools were deep, maybe twenty feet or more, and the water would still be icy in them. He promised himself to come back and visit them again someday.

The trail turned steeply uphill and gave Dan a view up the canyon. He wondered if the osprey would make an appearance now, but he knew it was probably too early. The fish wouldn't be rising up out of the depths of the pools until the sun was lower in the sky, and the osprey certainly knew this. He knew how to get his own dinner.

And then Dan was at the trailhead, into a chaotic scene of emergency vehicles.

He hadn't expected this. Radios gargled. Men in uniform were everywhere, surrounded by a sea of cars and flashing lights. The whole area had been cordoned off.

And they hadn't expected him. A couple of officers came over quickly to challenge him, but it didn't take Dan long to get free of them. Now the challenge was getting his car out. One of the officers finally had to move a van so that Dan could make his way past the yellow tape barrier. Another officer waved him out onto the highway.

There was no traffic. Dan pulled out onto the road and drove off. A quick check in his rearview mirror showed a kaleidoscope of lights and vehicles behind him.

It wasn't until he was over the summit and driving down the mountain past Lake Alpine that his phone started beeping at him, messages from the past two days. He decided that he wasn't interested, but glanced for a moment at the screen and saw that there were messages, lots of messages, including some from Kristen.

Dan kept driving, but the messages began to wear his resistance down. He found a wide spot in the road and pulled over to check.

No service.

Dan plugged his phone into the charger in his car and drove

another few miles. When it pinged again, he pulled over and found that he had service.

The first message was from Cal Healey. It was short and to the point. Dan should give him a call when he got a chance.

Then a second message from Cal, more urgent. Please call ASAP.

The third message from Cal, explaining that the prints on the bear can were identified as being from Donald Lamar Graham, a violent criminal wanted on several charges including murder.

Dan should not go hiking in Mokelumne Canyon, and if he were down there, he should get the hell out.

Dan checked the time on that last message. It was a little before ten o'clock yesterday morning. That would explain the deputies arriving later that afternoon.

He tapped the phone to get the next message. It was Steve Matson, telling him to call into the office immediately. He would let that one wait for a while.

The fifth message was Kristen. "Dan, I just heard from Cal Healey. If you get this message, please call him immediately. It's urgent." She sounded worried. But Dan guessed that Cal hadn't told her the whole story. It was nice to hear her voice, and Dan felt a slight glow through his body, his muscles slowly letting go. He took a deep breath and allowed that to continue for a few moments.

He looked back at the phone. There were more messages. One from Doris, saying pretty much the same thing as the one from Kristen. Only, being Doris, she sounded even more worried.

How many more were there? He tapped again. This time it was Cal Healey. "Hey buddy, glad to hear that you're okay. Give me a call when you get back into town and I'll bring you up to speed. And you can tell me all about it. Really glad you're okay. Really glad."

That was the last message. Dan ran through the messages again, this time deleting all of them except the one from Kristen. That one he'd like to hear again sometime.

He put the phone down and leaned back in his seat. It was quiet, and Dan opened up the windows. A slight breeze blew through the cab. He wasn't sure how long he stayed that way, but eventually he heard a noise, the slow moan of an approaching car. Dan waited for it to reach him and roar by.

Then he started the engine and drove home.

chapter 44

By the time Dan got back to his house above Sonora, it was late afternoon. He grabbed his gear and brought it inside, took a quick look at his mail—nothing there to worry about—and got ready to take a shower.

The phone rang, and before he even looked at it, he had decided that there was really only one person he would talk to right now: Kristen. Everybody else could wait.

When he looked at the phone, the caller ID showed Tuolumne County Sheriff's Department. Dan figured it could well be Cal Healey, but Cal could wait.

He stripped off his clothes and took a long, hot shower.

When he came out, his phone showed three more calls, one from Cal's cell phone, one from the Mi-Wuk Station, and one from Kristen.

He clicked on the one from Kristen and called her back.

It made Dan smile to her hear voice. "Hi, Dan! How are you?"

They exchanged a few pleasantries, and Dan figured out that Kristen didn't know the details of the last two days. She was just calling to make sure he was okay, because Cal Healey was looking for him and he had sounded concerned.

Dan was happy just listening to her talk, but she eventually turned the conversation to him, and he gave her a very short version of what had happened. "We ran into some wacko down there who shot Chris. But the cavalry arrived just in time, and I got out today without any trouble."

"Oh, my God!" Kristen was horrified. "Is Chris all right?"

Which was something Dan didn't know. He explained about the chopper and said that he needed to call the hospital to find out about Chris.

Of course, Kristen wanted to know more, and by the time they hung up, he had told her more than just the bare bones of the story: about Alex and the gunman, and the Sheriffs arriving. And the fact that at one point he was looking at a guy who was pointing a rifle at him from about thirty feet away with every expectation of killing him.

As he got to this point in the story he had trouble talking. His throat was tightening, and he couldn't keep going. He squeezed out a few words of apology to Kristen and tried to hang up, but not before she insisted that he needed to call Cal. It was really important.

Dan blurted out something that almost sounded like "Okay, I will, bye," and hung up.

He collapsed down onto his sofa and stared at his phone. He didn't have the strength to call Cal right now. But Kristen had reminded him that he wanted to check on Chris, too.

They had probably taken him to the hospital in Sonora, so Dan tried to pull himself together and called there. Of course, they told him that they couldn't release any patient information to anyone except the family. Dan tried to pretend that his call was official USFS business, but that got him nowhere. Patient privacy took precedence, he was informed.

Dan stared at the phone again. He could try to call Chris directly but decided against that. What if...well, he didn't want to do that.

He didn't want to call Chris' family and have them tell him Chris didn't make it. That's what he didn't want.

So, he called Cal Healey.

"Jesus!" Cal answered the phone. "Are you okay?" The concern in his voice was palpable.

"Yeah, I'm fine," Dan tried to assure him. "But I was hoping you might be able to give me an update on Chris Martin. How is he doing?"

"Is he the guy who got shot?" Cal asked. "Last I heard, they medivac-ed him here to the hospital, but I don't know more than that."

"Any chance you could find out for me?" Dan asked. "I'd really like to know, and I don't want to bother his family."

"Probably," Cal admitted, somewhat dubiously. "Part of the investigation and all…"

Dan took a deep breath and let it out slowly.

"Are you doing okay?" Cal asked. "From what I heard, it got pretty damn hairy down there."

"Yeah, it did," Dan agreed. "But I'm okay. I got out fine."

"Sounds like you're the only one," Cal said.

"Yeah," Dan agreed quietly. He hadn't thought about it that way.

They let the silence hang there for a minute or two. Then they both started talking at once. Dan started to mention the deputies arriving, and Cal to suggest that he would call the hospital.

Another pause, and Cal suggested Dan go first.

"It was just a damn good thing that those deputies got there when they did," he said. "Otherwise, I think we would have really been fucked. Especially Chris."

"Well, I'm glad that worked out," Cal said. "When you didn't pick up your phone or answer your messages, I got worried."

"We were down there in the canyon," Dan said. "No way to get service down there."

"Yeah, I know," Cal said. "But what you didn't know was that we got those prints off your bear can. Armed, violent and dangerous. Mr. Donald Lamar Graham. That was bad news. He was bad news."

"Wait," Dan stopped him. "Did you call in those deputies?"

"Well, I just told Calaveras County where that guy Graham might be—and that there were innocent people in the area."

"Shit, Cal!" Dan exploded. "Thanks, man. You just saved my life…"

Cal chuckled. "That's not the way I heard it. But yeah, I suggested they get their ass down there… and they did."

Dan started to thank Cal again when Cal interrupted him. "I'm gonna call the hospital for you now. I'll get back to you in a few minutes. Then you can tell me all about what a great guy I am."

Dan leaned back into the sofa. He thought he should probably do something about dinner. He was hungry after the light lunch on the trail and the hike out.

He walked into the kitchen and opened the door of the fridge. Not much there, but with a couple of eggs and a little cheddar cheese he could make an omelet. And he had bread to toast. Nothing much in the way of vegetables. Maybe he'd have a pickle and pretend that would serve.

As he filled his hands with food, the phone rang again. He answered it quickly without looking. He was disappointed to discover it was Steve Matson.

"Calling to make sure you're okay," he said to Dan.

"I'm okay," Dan said. "I'm fine. I guess the whole world knows about it, huh?"

"We generally hear about it when one of our rangers gets shot," Matson agreed. "Do you want to talk about it at all?"

"Not really," Dan said. "I'm kinda tired and hungry."

"If you need a day or two, let me know," his boss said. "I'm fine with that, given the circumstances."

"Thanks, Steve. I think I'll be fine." Dan answered.

"You weren't down there doing trail work, were you?" Matson asked him.

Dan looked at his phone. "Hey Steve, this is Cal Healey on the other line. I better take this call."

Matson signed off by repeating his offer to give Dan a day or two to recover.

It was another fifteen minutes before Cal called.

"Chris lost a lot of blood," he said. "They are calling it critical but stable condition. Sounds like they got him out in time, and he'll be okay."

"What about Alex?" Dan asked.

"She's already been released. Headed back home with her mom," Cal answered.

Which was about as good as might be expected.

"The perp is still in a coma, and they're not sure about him," Cal continued. "I know you're not necessarily pulling for him, neither am I, but I thought you'd want to know."

"Yeah. Thanks," Dan said. "I guess Alex hit him pretty hard."

"Yeah, even if he does come out of it, they say they don't know if he can recover completely," Cal agreed.

"Well, thanks for the update," Dan said.

"Oh, one more thing before I forget," Cal added. "I think they found those loppers."

Cal waited for a reaction from Dan. He didn't get one. "I figured you'd want to know, government property and all," Cal continued.

"Yeah, thanks, Cal. Very nice." Dan said as sarcastically as possible. And then, much more seriously. "Hey, thank you, for what you did."

"Get some food and rest," Cal ignored Dan's comments. "You need it."

Dan put the phone down and cracked a couple of eggs into a bowl and tossed a pat of butter into the frying pan on the stove.

chapter 45

It was a few days later that the phone rang around dinner time.

Dan checked to see it was Chris Martin calling and answered with a warm greeting. "Hey Chris! How are you doing?"

But it wasn't Chris on the phone. It was Chris' wife Donna. She explained that Chris was home from the hospital and doing well. In fact, he was planning to try to go into work next week, although she thought that was a terrible idea.

"But that's not why I called," she continued. "I wanted to thank you, personally, for what you did up there in Mokelumne Canyon."

Dan resisted her implication that he had been the hero of the day. "I think we ended up being a pretty good team, after all." he said. "We didn't plan it that way, but that's how it happened."

"Well, I want to thank you again," Donna said. "In person. And I won't take no for an answer. I'm inviting you for lunch sometime next week. You pick the day that would be best for you."

Dan grinned. He would be delighted to see Chris and check in on him again. And Donna sounded like someone he'd like to know anyway. "Sure, that sounds like fun," he said. He checked his calendar quickly. "Does Thursday work for you?"

"Perfect!" Donna enthused. "Come around noon and we'll eat whenever you get here. And please bring a guest if you'd like."

Dan wondered if Kristen would be able to join him. He wrote

down their address and then asked if he could speak to Chris.

Donna laughed. "He's out for a short walk. I had to wait for him to leave to do this. But you guys can talk later. Or all Thursday afternoon, if you want."

Which was how Dan and Kristen found themselves driving into Markleeville that following Thursday, looking for the Martins' house. With a little help from Google, they found it, just outside of town, a smaller A-frame chalet with a large deck out in front. It was set back from the road, and as Dan looked around, he guessed that most of the lots in the area were about an acre. Lots of room, he thought approvingly.

As they drove up the gravel driveway, they could see Chris moving around out on the deck between a couple of umbrellas.

Chris waved as they got out of the car, and waved them on up to the deck, his left arm still in a sling.

He and Dan shook hands warmly, big grins on their faces. Then it was time for introductions all the way around as Dan met Donna, and introduced Kristen to everyone.

Donna called for Alex to come down and join them, and a few minutes later she did, quietly, and sat down at the far end of the table that Donna had set for lunch, quickly engrossed in her phone.

Dan asked about their other daughter. "At school. Cal Poly," Chris said. "We see her about once every two months, when she runs out of money," and laughed.

"Sounds like when I was in school," Dan said.

"She offered to come home," Chris said. "But I told her with the money I was spending, I'd rather have her in class."

Donna thanked Dan for coming, then went into the kitchen to bring out the food. When she heard that Kristen ran a catering business, she quickly started apologizing for the food, but Kristen cut her off. "Someone else cooking for me is the ultimate luxury," she said. "It doesn't get any better."

During lunch, Donna quizzed Dan about the events down in the canyon, but after a few minutes Chris called a halt to that line of questioning. "I don't think we should go into that today," he said. "We lived it. We don't need to relive it."

Donna consented, a bit reluctantly, and Chris turned the conversation to trail work. Soon he and Dan were deep into a conversation about how they might tackle the massive job of opening up the old trails that had been created decades or more ago, and who might help with that other big tree.

By the time dessert was on the table, the two men had shared stories about their various conversations with their supervisors in the USFS, and the lack of money for any kind of improvements to infrastructure.

"Hell, we can't even keep up what we have now," Chris insisted. "We aren't going to see any money spent on new trails."

What followed was a long conversation about how much work would actually be required, and how many people it would take to get it done.

Dan wrapped up the discussion. "You and me, Chris," he said. "We're the ones who may have to make it all happen. And a few thousand volunteers."

"That's what we need!" Chris said. "I should get Alex to work on that: a crowdsourcing campaign for trail work."

They shot a glance at Alex, who paid them no attention. She was deep in conversation with Kristen at the other end of the table, their two heads close together.

Dan was happy to see the two women getting along so well. Donna joined them at the mention of crowdsourcing.

"The girls have started a campaign to help with our bills," she said. "This whole thing doesn't qualify for worker's comp. So the two of them got to work on that."

Chris smiled. "Mainly supported right now by donations from a few people in the Forest Service, but there's a fundraiser in the works over at the local church."

"Wait a minute," Dan said. "Wasn't that guy Graham on the Most Wanted list? Doesn't the FBI have some kind of a reward program for those guys?"

Chris gave a rueful smile. "Apparently, there's some discussion about exactly where on that list he was at the time. But yeah, that might be an option. We'd split it with you fifty-fifty."

Dan snorted. "Fuck that. First of all, there were two of you and only one of me. And secondly, I don't have any medical expenses or anything. You use it to pay off whatever you need."

This brought another sermon of gratitude from Donna, who followed it up with a third offer of coffee. "Since you have a drive ahead of you, I thought you might need some," she suggested to Dan.

Dan looked at Kristen, still in conversation with Alex. He caught her eye briefly, and a nod.

"I think we'd better hit the road," he said. "It is a long drive...."

On the way home, Kristen was quieter than usual. Dan was enjoying the drive, basking in the sun and the memories of their lunch on the deck. As they drove down Highway 395 he began to talk about Chris and Donna and their house. And he talked away. He was still talking as they climbed up towards Sonora Pass on Highway 108.

"You seemed to get along really well with Alex," he said to Kristen. "That was great."

Kristen was silent, looking out the side window as Dan drove. As he turned off onto 108 to come over the pass, he glanced at Kristen. Tears were running down her face.

"Are you okay?" he asked with concern.

Kristen nodded, but said nothing, which didn't put Dan's mind at ease.

The curves on the road over the pass quickly demanded his attention, and it was hard for him to follow up.

"What's wrong?" he asked. "Is it Alex? She seems to be recovering okay." This was more of question than a statement.

Kristen looked out the window again, then sniffed and wiped her eyes.

"Is she doing okay?" Dan asked.

"About what you would expect," Kristen admitted, quietly.

Dan thought about this. "Well, it was great that you could talk to her. You seemed to really be able to connect with her."

"She has a very long road ahead," Kristen said. And then, after a pause, "It was for me."

The words hit Dan like a truck. It was all he could do to keep the vehicle on the road.

And he didn't know what to say. Should he say he was sorry? About what? What had happened in Kristen's past? And what could he possibly say?

"I don't know what to say, Kristen," Dan choked out. "I had no idea. I am sorry..."

She shook her head, then looked out the window, and they drove along again in silence.

Dan's mind was racing, wondering if there was something he could or should do to help. And he didn't know the answer. He couldn't think of anything that seemed right. He thought of taking her hand, but even touching her seemed too aggressive, too much of an imposition on her space.

That, and he was driving on a twisting road through the mountains. Not a good time to take one hand off the wheel.

"I'm sorry," he said again. "I didn't know. I don't know what to say or do. I'm completely at a loss."

By now they were up at the top of the pass. Trails from here led north to Tahoe, and south to Yosemite and beyond, all along the crest of the Sierra.

Kristen pointed ahead to the parking area beneath Sonora Peak. "Could we stop there for a minute?" she asked.

Dan immediately turned into the parking area and pulled to a stop.

Kristen opened her door and started walking towards the outhouse at the far side of the parking lot.

Dan couldn't decide if he should get out or not. He somehow felt strongly that she needed space right now. But at the same time, that space excluded him, and he wanted to help her any way that he could. He finally decided to get out of the car and go sit at a nearby picnic table.

When he glanced over to check on Kristen, he was surprised to see that she hadn't entered the outhouse. Instead, she had walked past it, and was now standing on the far side, arms wrapped around herself, staring down the west side of the pass.

Dan let her stand there for what seemed like a long time. Ten minutes? Fifteen? Maybe more.

He decided to walk over to her, and stood next to her, a few feet away, joining her in looking down into the valley.

They stood there, next to each other, for another few minutes.

As she stared off into the distance, Kristen finally spoke. "I choose to be with you, Dan," she said quietly and turned to look at him. "It's my decision."

Dan smiled. "Me, too," he said. "Thank you," and reached out a hand.

She took his hand, and they walked back to the truck together.

chapter 46

That night when he dropped Kristen off at her home, he kept his distance. She leaned over in the seat and kissed him quickly on the cheek as she got out of the truck.

They both understood that it would take time to work through this. Dan wished her goodnight and drove back to his house. It seemed cold and dark when he got there.

The next day he was back at work at the Summit Ranger Station. He knew it would busy, as Fridays often were. Lots of people arriving in time to get out on the trail or find a campsite before the real crowds arrived later in the afternoon.

Dan welcomed the distraction of so many people. They took his mind off his relationship with Kristen, and the events of the previous days.

Doris was a few minutes late. That wasn't like her, but there were already people inside the lobby by the time she arrived. She waved to Dan, took her spot behind the counter, and started talking almost before she had stopped walking in from her car.

It wasn't until half-past ten that things slowed down a bit.

Dan had already told Doris all about the adventures down in Mokelumne Canyon, but it was her turn now to give him some news. And with their staggered days off, it was the first time they were working together in a week.

"Did you hear about what happened in the parade?" she asked him.

This was going to be news to Dan. He normally didn't follow those kinds of events

He told Doris that he didn't even know there was a parade.

"It was a special event for the state park in Columbia…their big anniversary parade," she explained.

Dan said that he was sorry to have missed it.

Doris waved her hand dismissively at him. She wasn't buying it. "No, you're not," she said. "But I was there because Travis was going to be in it." Travis was her grandson, and in the eyes of Doris was the most remarkable young man on planet Earth.

"Cool!" Dan said. "Was he in costume or something?"

Doris gave a sigh. "He was part of an a capella singing group at the high school," she said happily. "They were singing old mining songs."

Dan laughed. "That sounds like it would be fun."

"But that's not what happened," Doris said. "I mean, they sang the songs, and they were great. But some other kids got themselves into a world of trouble."

She stopped here to give her words full impact.

Dan waited patiently for the story to continue.

"There were some kids that had built some kind of float for the parade," Doris continued. "You know, with flowers and decorations and things? And they were driving that right in the parade. Right in front of Cal Healey, who was there driving his squad car."

Dan smiled. "I bet Cal loved that. Did he have the siren going and the lights flashing?"

"At first, just the lights," Doris said. "And then he started with the siren. People were covering their ears."

Dan shook his head and chuckled. "Sounds like Cal's sense of humor."

"But he was serious!" Doris exclaimed. "It wasn't part of the parade. He was trying to stop those kids with their float."

Dan looked at her. "That doesn't sound like Cal," he said. "He doesn't usually like to ruin a good parade."

"No, it wasn't the parade," Doris explained. "It was the car. The car in the float. It was Carol Lawlor's car!"

chapter 47

Dan waited until he got home that night to call Cal.

"I understand that you solved the mystery of the reappearing car," he said to Cal.

Cal wasn't amused. "What a circus that was," he said.

"Well," Dan continued. "I'm proud of you. Taking dangerous criminals off the street is important work. And you did it while you were marching in the parade."

He waited for Cal's reaction.

"Driving, but yeah," Cal said. "And nobody is off the streets."

"Juvenile Court?" Dan asked.

"Oh, it's worse than that," Cal answered. "They don't even want to press charges."

"What do you mean?" Dan asked. "Who doesn't?"

"That lawyer with the non-profit," Cal said. "Turns out the gang of car thieves was three kids from the local high school auto shop class. They had been given an assignment by their teacher—to develop a security system for a Camry."

Dan started laughing. "That's a long way from stealing a Camry."

"Yeah," Cal agreed. "But once they understood how easy it was to steal one, they decided to have some fun."

Dan thought about this. "It's still auto theft, though, right?"

"Yep. Except every time they stole the car, they did something else to fix it up. Changed the oil. Bought a new battery. Detailed the interior. Put better tires on it. The last time, they even put in a better sound system so that they could have music for their float in the parade."

"You're kidding?" Dan laughed out loud. "All of that on a stolen car?"

"Oh, yeah," Cal confirmed. "They were having so much fun working on this car that they got a little careless, or we might never have caught them."

"So what's going to happen to them?" Dan asked.

"We all had a nice long talk down at the high school," Cal said. "The auto shop teacher was a pretty good defense attorney. They're suspended for the summer, whatever that means. And under very close supervision for next year."

"Whew!" Dan let out a gasp. "They got lucky."

"Yeah," Cal agreed. "And the lawyer decided that he would donate the car to the auto shop program at the high school. Which means we'll probably be seeing that damn car in the parade every year."

"Geez," he teased Cal "So much for Grand Theft Auto. Seems like the really bad guys always get off."

"I'm just glad I don't have to keep tracking down that fucking car," Cal said.

"I thought you were having fun with that," Dan teased him.

"You know what I have fun with?" Cal asked him. "I was tracking down some of this stuff with your friend Mr. Graham."

Even now, hearing the name gave Dan a delicate feeling in his stomach.

"What did you find out?" he asked.

"They're still working through all the evidence they found down there," Cal said, referring to Mokelumne Canyon. "But they already did find some interesting stuff."

"Like what?" Dan asked.

"Like a Boy Scout knife, complete with both the troop number and the scout's last name," Cal said. "They tracked that down to an Eagle Scout who disappeared two years ago. They don't know where he went, or what happened to him, but somehow this guy Graham ended up with his knife, so that's not good."

"You might talk to Chris Martin about that," Dan suggested. "That would fit with a timeline of some stuff he found up above the canyon a while back."

"Okay," Cal replied. "Boy, you are a regular fountain of information. Anything else you are keeping back?"

"Got me," Dan answered. "If something comes to me, I'll let you know."

"They also found some remains down there," Cal said. "Looks like they are probably Carol Lawlor—the lady from the bookstore."

"Oh," Dan let out a groan. "That's too bad. That will really hit Doris hard."

"Yeah, well, ready for the punchline?" Cal asked. "Turns out that Carol did have a next of kin. Donald Lamar Graham was her second cousin, or step-cousin or something. Anyway, they were related."

Dan thought about the femur that he had picked up down in the canyon. He hoped that it was from a deer.

Cal signed off and Dan put his phone down.

He wondered if anyone had told Doris about Carol yet. Somebody should. And he knew who that somebody should be.

With a sigh, he looked at his phone.

chapter 48

It was getting dark outside.

Dan knew it wouldn't take long for news to travel around this small community. With another sigh, he picked up his phone and dialed Doris' number.

Doris was quick to pick up. "Hi, Dan!" she bubbled over the phone. In the background, Dan thought he heard other voices.

"Did I interrupt something?" he asked. "Do you have guests?"

"The kids are over here," Doris explained. "Cynthia had to run some errands, so I am watching them do their homework."

Dan could hear a young girl giggling in the background. "Doesn't sound much like work to me," he said.

He heard Doris say something to her granddaughter and the giggling stopped.

"I am sorry, Doris," Dan said. "but I have some bad news." And he told her about Carol.

Doris was silent for a while, and they sat with each other on the phone. Dan heard a little voice ask Grandma a question, and he heard Doris sniff before answering in a quiet voice, "Nothing, honey, Grandma just found out some bad news about a friend of hers."

"I'm sorry Doris," Dan said. "I wish the news was different. But I thought you'd want to know."

"Yes, you're right," Doris said. "Thank you, Dan." Another silence followed.

Dan asked if there was anything he could do for her. And he knew the answer before she gave it. She was with her granddaughter, and that was probably the best thing for now.

Dan started to say good-bye when Doris interrupted him.

"I'm sorry, but I forgot to tell you," she said. "Kristen called just after you left today. She said it wasn't important, but I thought you should know."

"I'll call her," Dan promised.

"She didn't really leave a message, Dan," Doris explained. "She didn't ask you to call her back. I'm not even sure that she told me who she was…"

"Okay," Dan agreed. "I'll still call her."

"But I think she wanted to talk to you," Doris continued.

Dan smiled. "Got it, Doris. I will call her. I promise. As soon as we hang up."

"I think that would be best," Doris said. "And thank you again, for telling me about Carol. It's very sad. But call Kristen."

After the call, Dan stared at the phone, shaking his head. There were times that he really didn't know what to do with Doris. But he kept his promise, and dialed Kristen's number.

Kristen sounded surprised to hear from him.

"I had a conversation with Doris just now, and she suggested that I call you," Dan explained. And he went on to tell her about Carol Lawlor.

"People can be so horrible," Kristen said to him. "It's hard to imagine why."

Dan agreed, and was about to say something more when Kristen interrupted him.

She told him that she was quite busy with work, but that she had called to see if he might want to join her for dinner on Wednesday night.

That sounded good to Dan. "I think that sounded like an invitation," he said to her. "If it is, I'd like to accept it."

"Yeah," Kristen responded. He could tell from the sound of her voice that she was smiling. "It was an invitation to dinner. Is that okay?"

"It's great," Dan said. "When and where?"

"Nothing special," Kristen said. "I'll just cook something for us here at home. About six?"

"Perfect," Dan said. "What can I bring? Wine? Dessert?" In the back of his mind he was thinking about a nice bouquet of flowers.

"Nope," Kristen answered. "I think I have it all here. All you need to bring is you."

afterword

Dan was nearing the end of his hike down the granite bench of the canyon. Here was where the route might get tricky. He stopped for a moment to stare up at the searing blue sky freckled with a few small puffy white clouds higher up the canyon. There was a gentle breeze now picking up from the west and Dan felt it soften the heat of the day, cooling him as it wafted the sweat off his arms and face.

To his relief, the slope at the far end of the bench was gentle, just the way it looked on the map, with no surprises. Two simple ledges led one into the other, and Dan didn't even need to pick his way along. The route was obvious. That bench had been like a massive granite freeway taking him down into the very heart of the gorge.

At the base of the bench, Dan found a small cascade, the water gushing over a lip in the rock into a deep, shady pool hiding between huge boulders. And looking downstream, Dan could see that the gradient eased, and the river now meandered along through the forest, offering both shade and scattered beams of sunlight, glittering on the water. Compared to the sunbaked granite he had just hiked, it was an oasis of shade, forest, and cold water.

It had been a long hike.

Dan gave a huge sigh and dropped his pack against a log in a large clearing beside the deep pool. This was certainly the right place. He noted the flat areas that would be perfect to pitch a tent or two, and the ancient fire ring with a couple of now almost rotten logs pulled together as seating, now worn shiny by years of use.

After resting for a few minutes, he opened up his pack, took out his water filter, and walked down to the edge of the pool. He saw a few small trout scatter as he approached the water, racing upstream into the depths of the pool. That was a good sign. The bigger fish would be invisible down there, deeper in the pool. They would only come up during the cool of the evening to take his flies. He set up his water filter and began to pump, slowly, into his bottles.

As he settled into this ritual, sitting on the edge of the river, he heard the cry of an osprey. A moment later it sailed into view, slowly drafting down the canyon above the river. He stopped pumping and sat back to watch it soar silently overhead and then continue past him, above the trees and off into the distance down the gorge, its white feathers gleaming in the sunlight.

He filled up two water bottles, took them back uphill to his campsite, and sat down on a log next to his pack. He pulled out his bear canister and rummaged around, looking for a snack to enjoy.

"Hey," a voice called out from behind him. "Looks like you made it!"

Chris Martin walked into the clearing from the far end, wearing a backpack and a big smile.

"I did indeed," Dan answered. "It was a pretty great hike."

"Mine too," Chris said, gingerly setting his pack next to Dan's. He was still favoring that left arm, Dan noted.

"How's the shoulder?" Dan asked.

Chris gently moved his left arm around in a circle. "Not bad," he said. "Kind of like the trail back there. Still needs some work, but it's definitely getting better."

Chris took a moment to look around. "This is a nice spot," he said, nodding appreciatively.

Dan grinned and pointed to the huge granite bench above them. "It's got lots of parking, too."

"I see that," Chris said. He turned and looked at Dan, then held out his hand. "Nice to meet you here."

Dan shook Chris' hand and smiled. "We made it," he said.

"We sure as hell did," Chris agreed. "We made it… and," he added, pointing to the trail he had just walked, "we made that, too. All the way through. It now connects all the way, one end to the other."

Dan grinned. "More or less. Still needs some work. But yeah, we did."

Chris sat down next to Dan and dug around in his pack for a few minutes. "They always need more work, Dan. That's why we have jobs." With a grunt he sat back and pulled out a bag and offered it to Dan.

"Want some grapes?"

ALSO AVAILABLE:

When a Wall Street tycoon insists that his family join him for an annual backpacking trip into the Sierra Nevada, some of his children are not enthusiastic about the idea.

And that's before people start turning up dead. Ranger Dan Courtwright is first on the scene. And with his friend Sheriff Cal Healey, he sticks with it to the terrifying finish, which is a real cliffhanger. Literally.

DANGER: FALLING ROCKS is available on Amazon.com.

Acknowledgments

Most of my books are invented, whole cloth, from my memories of adventures in the mountains, both real and imagined. But this book has drawn on tales told to me by others, as well. I want to thank Chip Morrill for telling his tales, and for being both a good friend and a great trail crew manager. Bill King is the same kind of person, and I am grateful for his stories and trail crew work as well. And the tale of Monty Wolfe is no tale at all. I owe a debt of gratitude to Veda Guild Linford, who shared her manuscript about Monty Wolfe, who just happens to be her grandfather. I hope she eventually will publish it, as it is a wonderful bit of fun. Mary Matzek shared her own knowledge of Monty and put me in contact with Veda. Robin Lewis is a prince and manages the design and production of these books with patience and style.

Karen Johnson added her wonderful suggestions to the text, as have both of my daughters, Liz and Estelle. Finally, a note of thanks to my wife, Margaret, who is kind enough to proof my work, and tries to keep me from making the most egregious errors. She is often successful.